SUMMER BLOWOUT

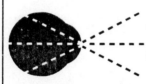

This Large Print Book carries the
Seal of Approval of N.A.V.H.

SUMMER BLOWOUT

CLAIRE COOK

THORNDIKE PRESS

A part of Gale, Cengage Learning

GALE
CENGAGE Learning

Detroit • New York • San Francisco • New Haven, Conn • Waterville, Maine • London

GALE
CENGAGE Learning

LIBRARY OF CONGRESS CATALOGING-IN-PUBLICATION DATA

Cook, Claire, 1955–
   Summer blowout / by Claire Cook.
     p. cm.
   ISBN-13: 978-1-4104-0986-7 (hardcover : alk. paper)
   ISBN-10: 1-4104-0986-4 (hardcover : alk. paper)
    1. Beauty operators—Fiction. 2. Large type books. I. Title.
PS3553.O55317S86 2008
813'.54—dc22   2008021661

Published in 2008 by arrangement with Hyperion, an imprint of Buena Vista Books, Inc.

Printed in the United States of America
1 2 3 4 5 6 7 12 11 10 09 08

TO MY READERS

ACKNOWLEDGMENTS

Lisa Bankoff is not only the world's best literary agent, but on the phone one day she even confessed her own lipstick addiction, which was just tailor-made for this novel. I never did find a way to get Shu Uemura #265E in there, but heartfelt thanks all the same. And a huge thank-you to Tina Wexler, too, for always being there with kind words and keen insight.

Speaking of dynamic duos, Ellen Archer and Pamela Dorman are just the best! I'm so happy to see Voice take off, and thrilled to get to go along for the ride. I'm particularly grateful for a brainstorming luncheon at Café Nougatine with Ellen, Pam, and oh-so-wonderful associate editor Sarah Landis, where the advice might have been even better than the food, and where my brilliant editor Pam Dorman turned a beauty book into a beauty kit with a wave of her magic wand.

I keep threatening to apply for a real job at Voice because I'm just so crazy about everybody there. Jane Comins and Jessica Wiener have been honest and forthcoming, and I've learned so much from them. Alex Ramstrum is a truly amazing publicist, and I'm so lucky to have Beth Gebhard's Southern charm behind me, too. I could write a book about how wonderful each and every person at Voice has been, but they'd probably prefer I write a real book instead, so I'll settle for sending a great big alphabetical thanks to Anna Campbell, Kathleen Carr, Christine Casaccio, Rachel Durfee, Maha Khalil, Laura Klynstra, Claire McKean, Lindsay Mergens, Karen Minster, Shelly Perron, Mike Rotondo, and Sarah Rucker.

A million thanks to Charlotte Phinney for being kind and generous enough to guide me through the mysterious world of hair and makeup for this novel, for letting me shadow her, for answering an endless barrage of questions, and for some great laughs.

Thanks, too, to Tanya, Stacey, Helena, Pam, Maria, and the whole gang at Pipeline Salon, to Phoebe and Elaine at Phoebe's Faces, to Donna Harlow of Harlow's Hair Design, and to Donna Crowley of Charles David Salon for inspiration and support.

Just about every time I mentioned this novel at one of my *Life's a Beach* book tour events, a hairstylist would take the time to come up afterward to express enthusiasm and maybe even offer a few tips. I'm sorry I didn't think to write down everybody's names, but your excitement really propelled me forward in the writing of this book, and I'm so grateful to all of you, including Shane from Ann Arbor, Elaine Shapiro from Rhode Island, and Kathleen Cosgrove from Peacock Style and Color in Norwell.

A gigantic thank-you to the booksellers, librarians, and members of the media who have talked up my books and cheered me on. I'm so grateful for your support.

Many thanks to the talented Diane Dillon, the first flight attendant/author photographer I've ever heard of, for keeping my flight scenes on course even as she snapped my photo. Genius.

A big thanks to Ken Harvey for reading and offering some great advice along the way.

Thanks to my daughter, Garet, and her fiancé, Geoff, for Atlanta input, and to Garet for showing up for a visit with her eight-pound dog, Coco, who not only backed our big, bad Daisy Mei into a corner, but proceeded to worm her way into our hearts and this novel. Many thanks to my son, Kaden, for always being there with his creativity, wisdom, and computer savvy. Thanks to my seven sisters and brothers and one stepmother, bunches of nieces and nephews, and extended family, plus old and new friends, for love and book buzz — just tell me which character you want to be this time around, and I'll back you up!

A huge thanks, always, to my husband, Jake, for being first reader, wise counsel, and killer proofreader.

And finally, to my fabulous readers — thanks for giving me the best job ever!

1

Lipstick is my drug of choice. I grabbed a tube of Nars Catfight, a rich, semi-matte nude mauve, on my way out of the salon. Easy access to beauty products is one of the perks of the business.

There were lots of cars in the parking lot, but I saw him almost as soon as I pushed the door open. He was sitting in the driver's seat, leaning back with his eyes closed. I was surprised I couldn't hear that big fat snore of his all the way from here.

I was across the parking lot before I knew it. I had a large chocolate brown shoulder bag with me, and I swung it sideways to gain some momentum. Then I picked up speed and hurled it at the windshield as hard as I could.

My ex-husband jumped like he'd been shot and crashed his head into the window beside him. In that instant I understood every wronged woman who had ever run over her husband. Or cut off his penis. I could have killed him. Easily. And then gone back for seconds.

Craig was looking at me with real fear in his eyes. I liked it. He looked down at the ignition, maybe calculating his chances for escape. He reached for the button and lowered the window about two inches. "What the hell was that?" he asked through the crack.

"What the hell was *that?* What the hell are you doing here?"

"Sophia's car's in the shop," he actually said. "She needed a ride."

If there was a gene for getting it, my former husband had clearly been born without it. "You're pond scum," I said. "No, you're lower than pond scum. If there's anything lower than pond scum, you're it." I stretched forward and started picking up the contents of my shoulder bag, which were scattered all over the hood of Craig's stupid Lexus. He didn't even own it. It was leased. I hoped he got completely screwed when it was time to pay for the scratches.

My Nars Catfight, which had somehow ended up on the hood, too, twinkled up at me. I reached for it and covered my lips in slow, soothing strokes. A round hairbrush rolled to the pavement. I bent down and picked it up, then stood and pointed the sharp end at him. "Get off my father's property. Now."

Craig shook his head, like I was the one with the problem. "Bella, it's Sophia's father's property, too."

"Great," I said. "Let me go find him for you. Then he can be the one to kill you."

That did it. Even before he'd left one of my father's daughters for another one of his daughters, my father hadn't been too crazy about Craig, and he knew it. He started up the car. "Just tell Sophia I'm waiting down the street for her, okay?"

"Sure," I said. "I'm all over it."

Up until then, he'd been looking over my head or off to the side of my face. Now he looked me right in the eyes, just for a second. Despite myself, I felt a little jolt of something, possibly insanity. Embarrassing as it would be to admit it, I had this sudden crazy urge to keep him from driving away.

I rested one hand on the hood of the car. Craig flinched. "How're the kids?" I asked.

He put the car into drive. "They're not your kids, Bella," he said. "Forget about them."

I made it to my first gig in record time, possibly propelled by the smoke coming out of my ears. Then I waited. And waited.

I couldn't take it anymore. I fumbled in my makeup kit so I could sneak another quick fix. After some consideration, I decided Revlon Super Lustrous in Pink Afterglow was a good choice for a recently divorced brunette with green eyes and ivory skin who'd just attacked her ex-husband's car and had lips that were a lot dryer than they used to be.

The housekeeper came in again. "He's on the telephone right now," she said.

I rolled down my lipstick fast. I popped the top back on and tossed it into my makeup kit.

"Thanks," I said. I tried to be discreet, but I couldn't resist running my tongue along my lower lip, savoring the rush as the emollients kicked in. The thing about lipstick is that, unlike the rest of life, it never lets you down. At least for the first five minutes. And even when it wears off, there's still the never-ending quest for a better, longer-lasting shade to keep you going.

"Can I get you anything?" she asked.

I knew it wouldn't be polite to say, *Yeah, my client,* so I just shook my head. When the housekeeper turned to walk away, I could see that the seam in her panty hose was crooked beneath her tight khaki skirt. A black skirt might have been more forgiving, but with khaki it really ruined the whole effect. Who even wore panty hose anymore, and the extra points she should have gained for the effort were more than canceled out by the appearance of a crooked crack. Or a possible buttocks imbalance. Apparently she didn't have any friends working in the house. A good friend tells you when your crack looks crooked.

I looked at my watch again. If the governor-running-for-senator actually showed his face during the next five minutes or so, I'd just about make it to my next job. No wonder they'd pawned him off on me. Sophia, who was his regular makeup artist, was also the regular makeup artist for the senator running for reelection against him. Since they were having a pre-season televised brunch debate at Faneuil Hall at eleven, they both needed makeup at the same time. I would have picked the other guy, too.

I grabbed a round black Studio Tech foundation compact and opened it. Yup, it was still MAC NW25. Partly to kill time, and partly just in case he turned out to be lighter or darker than he looked in the newspapers and on television, I reached into my kit and pulled out NW23 and NW30. I should have checked in with Sophia, but we weren't exactly speaking.

I'd commandeered one of the bay windows in the library to arrange my makeup, and then I'd pulled a wing chair over in front of it. It was my best shot at getting some decent light in this mausoleum. The gold and maroon velvet drapes appeared to have been there since the Boston Tea Party. The dark, leathery books on the floor-to-ceiling shelves didn't look much newer either.

My cell phone vibrated and danced around inside my purse. I wouldn't normally answer it while I was on a job, but because the client wasn't there yet, I reached in and picked it up. "Hello," I whispered.

"He's off the phone now," the housekeeper's voice whispered back.

I held out my cell phone and looked at it, then put it back to my ear. "Great," I said.

"Can I get you some coffee?"

"Nope," I said. "But thanks for asking."

My stomach growled. Mario had brought in breakfast sandwiches for everybody this morning, but I'd forgotten to grab one on my way out of the salon. Craig's Lexus would probably have ended up wearing it anyway, so I supposed it didn't really matter.

Off and on for the last hour, I'd been eyeing a huge library ladder on rollers that hooked over a brass track way up near the ceiling. I walked over to it. I put one foot up on the second rung, gave a little push, and lifted my other foot off the floor. It was kind of like riding a very tall scooter. Maybe I could at least find a decent book to flip through while I waited. I wondered if Governor What's His Name had actually read any of these, or if a decorator had found them for him. Massachusetts didn't have a governor's mansion, so this was probably just an overpriced rental.

I was halfway down one wall and picking up speed, when the housekeeper cleared her throat behind me. I figured it would be undignified to say *Oops,* so I just braked with my free foot and climbed off. I pulled my periwinkle tank top down to meet my chocolate brown capris. "Nice to see you again," I said. Not for the first time I noticed that her upper lip could use a good waxing.

"He's almost here," the housekeeper said. "He said to tell you it only takes him four minutes."

I wasn't sure that was something he should be calling attention to in an election year, but I knew my place, so I didn't say anything.

"He's eating his eggs, then he'll brush. Then he'll have me call for the car. And then he'll be in." She looked over at the window where my stuff had been camped out almost as long as the dust in the drapes. "Are you sure you're all set for him?"

A man poked his head through the heavy wooden doorway. He took a minute to look me up and down, in that creepy way at least one teacher in every high school in America has been checking out his students since the beginning of time. I glared at him. He was shorter and paler than the governor, or at least the way I imagined the governor, probably only an NW15. His lips were chapped, and his skin looked a little flaky, too. Moisture starts from the inside, so upping his water intake and adding some fish oil capsules would be his best bet. Of course, class starts from the inside, too, and as far as I could see, he didn't have a prayer in that department.

He finally finished ogling me and put his hands in his pockets. "And what are you pretty gals up to in here?" he asked.

The housekeeper tugged at the waistband of her khaki skirt in a fruitless attempt to realign things behind her. "We're just waiting to give the governor a little touch of makeup before his interview," she said.

The man shook his head. "Makeup," he said. "Better him than me, I guess." He leaned back into the hallway. "Gals," he yelled. "Free makeup in the library. Any takers?"

The look I gave him should have curled his eyelashes, but he didn't appear to notice. An anorexic blond with the wrong shade of hair for her complexion strolled in, gave me a bored look, then walked back out. The man followed her. The housekeeper followed the man.

I stood alone.

Sometimes the makeup artist is like a rock star. She's the guru you've been searching for. She can help you change your looks and maybe even your life. Other times, the makeup artist is like a maid. The toughest part is that you never know which one it's going to be when you walk through the door. Clearly, I was not having a rock star kind of day so far.

I walked over to a shelf, closed my eyes, and grabbed a book. I was hoping for a good one, but it turned out to be something boring about torts. Whatever they are. For lack of a better idea, I balanced the book on top of my head and took a couple of long, gliding steps. In health class back in sixth grade, we'd actually had to practice this to improve our posture. In hindsight, it wasn't a bad idea. It's not makeup, but good posture can go a long way toward creating the illusion of beauty.

And not to be depressing, but aren't some of the best parts of life really just an illusion?

2

The funny thing about waiting is that you wait and you wait and you wait. And then, suddenly, time speeds up like crazy, and you're there.

The housekeeper walked in with the governor right behind her. "Three minutes," he said.

"I'd heard four" slipped out before I thought it through.

"I don't need much," he said as he plopped down in the chair. I realized the book was still on top of my head, not that either of them seemed to notice. I dipped my head and caught the book with one hand, then handed it to the housekeeper. She walked it over to the exact shelf where I'd found it. Maybe she'd been a librarian in her last life.

I draped the governor in a black makeup cape. I applied some Laura Mercier foundation primer with a triangular foam sponge. I was happy to see that my first instinct had been right. He was definitely a MAC NW25. I opened the compact fast and rubbed the other side of the sponge back and forth until it was coated, then started covering his face in long, quick strokes. Even though I was in a rush, I paid special attention to his ears. I mean, my reputation was at stake here. There's nothing worse than turning on the TV to see some guy with red or white ears.

I grabbed my MAC powder blush in Angel. In an uncharacteristic lack of judgment, MAC had discontinued this shade, but I'd bought up enough to last me forever, as long as I was careful. Nars Orgasm is a great blush, too, but I didn't want to give this guy the satisfaction. And Angel looks good on everyone, even politicians. I dabbed some right on the apples of his cheeks.

"That's not blush, is it?" the housekeeper asked.

"Of course not," I lied. "It's only bronzer."

She nodded. "He likes a good tan."

With guys like this, I'd learned to get the foundation and blush on fast and set it with some loose powder. Then, if I had time, I'd go back in and fine-tune. This guy could certainly use some concealer, since he had major dark circles under his eyes, and some serious discoloration at the inside corners of his eyes, not to mention the outside corners of his nose. But you have to pick your battles.

Sure enough, just a few pats with the powder, and he stood up. "Mirror," he said to the housekeeper.

"He wants a mirror," the housekeeper said to me.

I reached for my mirror and angled it up at the governor-running-for-senator. He nodded approvingly at himself. When he looked away from the mirror, he seemed to notice me for the first time. He reached for my hand and shook it. "I'd appreciate your vote in November," he said. Then he turned and started to walk away.

I was tempted to leave the black cape on him. It might even help him win the election, since it gave him a bit of a superhero vibe, I thought. But I grabbed it and pulled. A good makeup artist always removes the cape before her client goes on television.

Getting from the Back Bay to the new conference center in the South End was a nightmare, but at least there was plenty of parking. I grabbed a coffee on the first floor and followed the signs for the Summer College Fair.

"Sure, just stroll in whenever you feel like it, Bella," my brother, Mario, said.

"Yeah, make us do all the prep work," my sister, Angela, said.

"Nice of you to bring us some coffee," my half sister Tulia said, as if I couldn't see that she already had one right beside her.

I took a long slow sip of my coffee. "Nice to see you, too," I said when I finished. "At least most of you."

My half sister Sophia looked away. Apparently her candidate hadn't kept her waiting forever like mine had, since she'd managed to beat me over here. A sudden picture of Craig sitting outside with his Lexus idling so she wouldn't be late popped into my head.

I pushed it away. I fumbled in my bag and pulled out a tube of Dolce Vita. Ha.

"How'd it go, anyway?" Mario asked.

I gave my lips a quick fix before I answered. "Asshole," I said.

"Him or me?"

I smiled. Of all my siblings, Mario was my favorite. "Both."

Mario smiled back. "Did you airbrush him?"

"Nah," I said. "I didn't feel like carrying the spray gun. I had to park way down the street."

Mario shook his head. "He'll be a mess on HDTV. Next time, use it, okay? I pitch us with cutting edge airbrush makeup. It's what sets us apart."

I rolled my eyes.

Mario gave me one of his looks.

"Sorry," I said. "I didn't think it was that big a deal."

"Okay, but you're going to have to use it in here. We'll need to move fast."

Good thing I'd brought my airbrush stuff in with me. I knew Mario would never fire me, but he was definitely capable of making me run back to my car. "So, why exactly are they having makeup and nails at a college fair?"

Mario shrugged. "Apparently it's the new big thing to attract spoiled rich kids and their parents to higher education. I hear they've got a massage booth and a fortune-teller, too."

The family business had grown beyond the small chain of salons owned by our communal father. We also did on-site television hair and makeup in the greater Boston area, plus weddings, funerals, and pretty much anything else that came in. Since my life imploded about a year ago, I'd been hitting the road as a makeup artist on the days I didn't work at one of my

25

father's hair salons, usually Salon de Lucio, but sometimes Salon de Paolo, or one of the others. I needed the money, since I planned to stay single and reinvent myself in some totally fascinating though as yet undetermined way.

I took another long slug of my coffee and tried not to think, which was becoming one of my specialties. Mario combed his freckled fingers through his curly brown hair, then clapped his hands. "Okay, everybody. Here's the deal. I got us our full day rates, plus parking and supplies, so keep track of your sponges and cotton balls, and make sure I get your parking receipts. And I said we couldn't work legally without disposable mascara wands, and I certainly wasn't going to pay for them at thirty-nine cents a pop." He smiled. "Eventually they caved."

"You're good," I said. Mario was in charge of our on-site business.

"I don't see why I have to do nails," Tulia said. Tulia was a total flake. She also couldn't makeup her way out of a paper bag, since she only moonlighted for Mario when she was maxed out on her charge cards. I gave Mario a look.

He put his arm around Tulia. "You're lucky we're letting you near the nails," he said. "And remember, only the people who

26

want light colors in your line. The dark colors go to Angela — she's got a steady hand. And don't forget . . ." Mario flipped through his stack of cosmetology licenses. "If anybody asks, you're Joanne Dolecheck."

"Whatever," Tulia said.

Technically, if you were not in a salon setting, the Massachusetts Cosmetology Board had no jurisdiction, but if you ran a business for our father, you always went the extra mile. It was part of the deal.

Loud music suddenly blasted out, and we could barely hear one another speak. Which was actually more than fine with me. I looked around. College banners draped the fronts of rows and rows of tablecloth-covered booths. Tweedy people stood behind them getting ready to pass out brochures and applications. I squinted. Some of the booths even sported displays of bottled water with the college name printed on them. Who knew.

Mario looked at his watch. "Places, everybody. The doors open at eleven."

I pulled out the extension legs on my case and set it up next to the first of the three hydraulic chairs Mario had brought in for the makeup applications. At the other end of the makeup chairs, Angela and Tulia were already seated at folding chairs and setting up nail polish and remover on top of two small round tables.

"I call lips," Jane said. Jane was our only makeup artist who was completely unrelated. Every so often we actually had to hire someone my father had neither married nor fathered.

"Okay," Sophia said. "I like eyes better anyway."

"I'm eyes, too," Mario said. "I think you're going to need me. I brought an extra folding stool, just in case."

"It'll be nice to see you doing some actual work for a change," I said. I reached for my airbrush gun and started setting it up. "And if I get ahead, I'll jump in and help out on lips."

I'd just turned the pressure up to forty and was blowing some MAC Micronized Airbrush Cleanser through my gun to make sure it wasn't clogged, when the guy at the booth next to me said, "Well, will you look at that."

He pointed. I looked. Way down in one corner of the ballroom, a wrestling ring with bright yellow ropes had been set up. A sumo wrestler in big white diapers adjusted a pile of giant padded sumo suits with flesh-colored torsos and limbs.

"Wow," I said. "I've always wanted to try

safe sumo wrestling."

"Yeah," the guy said. "Me, too." He paused. "Maybe we could check it out together later?"

"Excuse me?" I said. "You're not actually asking me to wrestle you, are you?"

"Just being neighborly," he said.

I turned to get a good look at him. He had large hazel eyes, thick hair and eyebrows, good skin, and a wide, slightly asymmetrical smile. If I hadn't given up on men for the rest of my natural life, I'd probably think he was cute, maybe even borderline supercute.

He reached out his right hand. "Hi," he said. "Sean Ryan."

"Is that first and middle or first and last?" I asked, not that it really mattered. "Bella," I added. "Bella Shaughnessy."

"Bella *Shaughnessy?*" he said, right before the doors opened and all hell broke loose. "What kind of name is that?"

3

A good makeup artist never panics, but I was close. I'd never seen so many high school kids and their parents in my entire life. The boys and the handful of fathers in attendance swarmed the sumo wrestling ring and formed long lines at the ultracaffeinated drinks booths. The girls and their mothers headed straight for either the massage people or us. The tweedy people at the college booths crossed their arms and waited. I guess they figured people would notice them eventually.

Angela and Tulia started right in on the nails. Angela had already given up on remover and was painting a darker color over an obviously stressed-out high school girl's chipped and well-bitten nails.

"Come on, Bella," Mario yelled from over where he was helping get the nail people separated into light color and dark color lines. "Do your thing so Sophia and Jane can get started on the eyes and lips."

I glanced out at the sea of faces. I picked up my airbrush gun. Airbrush makeup really was cutting edge. It was fast. It was accurate. It felt good going on. It stayed on until you decided to take it off. It could make even teenagers with bad skin look like porcelain dolls.

But cleaning out the gun between applications was a bitch. "Hey, Mario," I yelled. "Can you make some lines for us next?"

The woman right in front of me cleared her throat. She was probably an NW30. "Excuse me," she said. She made sure I saw her looking at her watch before she continued. "But how much longer are you going to be?"

"As long as it takes," I said. "Any other questions?"

That shut her up. One thing I've learned in my line of work is that people will walk all over you if you let them.

Mario finally came over. "What are you talking about?" he asked.

I waved my gun at the line and lowered my voice. "I was just thinking if you could line them up lighter to darker it would make things go much faster. That way I'd just have to keep adding drops of darker foundation, instead of cleaning out the gun and starting all over again between people."

"You want me to put the dark people at the back of the line? Are you crazy?"

I crossed my arms over my chest. "I'm just trying to be efficient here."

Mario put both hands on my shoulders and squeezed. "Bella, we can't do that. It's racial profiling."

"Ouch. It's not about race, it's about shade. I mean, you've already set a precedent with the nails. And they can go get a massage if they don't like it. It's not like they're paying. You just hate it when somebody else has a good idea."

The woman at the front of the line cleared her throat and looked at her watch again.

"Bella," Mario said. "This is Boston. We still haven't lived down busing in the seventies. Come on, get going or I'll take that gun away from you and use it myself."

Word was out on Tulia. "Excuse me," I heard her say to one girl, "but weren't you in my line?"

The girl pointed to Angela. "I want her," she said. "No offense, but you totally messed up my girlfriend's nails."

"Whatever," Tulia said. "Who's next?"

I'd opened my third bag of sponges a few faces ago. There were twelve to a pack, so that meant I'd done more than twenty-five foundation applications already. Before I primed and airbrushed, I was putting just a little bit of concealer on a sponge and applying that first. I hadn't taken the time for this step with the governor, but these poor kids had more than their share of zits, not to mention circles under their eyes from either studying or partying too hard. And their mothers looked even worse from all that worrying. The sponges also gave me an accurate count. In situations like these, at the end of the day I liked to know exactly how much I'd suffered.

I was so efficient I was causing a logjam for eyes and lips, so I took a minute to look over at the booth next door. That Sean Ryan guy had a pretty good line going for himself. He was handing out boxes of some kind and also doing a lot of nodding his head and joking with the parents and kids he was giving them to. I leaned over to try to get a better look, not at him, but at the boxes. He turned and looked at me. I looked away fast.

I was using a gravity-fed gun that had a little cup on the top for liquid foundation. If I had to go from a very dark face to a very light face, I emptied out the cup, turned on the gun, added some air gun cleaner, and then started all over again from square one. Otherwise, if the next face wasn't a big shade jump from the last one, I just figured out the difference and added a few drops to get the right shade for the next person. Then I held one finger over the end of the gun to block the air. This made it bubble, and the bubbles mixed the colors together.

"Hi," I said to the next girl in line. "What a pretty face you have." This wasn't completely true, but you never really knew who would grow into their looks and who wouldn't. Beauty is part facial symmetry, part surprise, part attitude. Plus, who couldn't use a compliment at that age. Or any age.

"Thank you," she said. The way she was beaming made me glad I'd exaggerated. Quickly I added a big squirt of NW35 to bring the NW25 in the cup up a few shades for her. I put my finger over the end of the gun.

"Wow, I know talent when I see it," Sean Ryan said beside me. "You're amazing."

I turned. The cup bubbled over. Polka dots of foundation spattered everybody in the immediate vicinity.

"Bella!" Jane screamed. Even the lipstick she was holding had polka dots on it.

"Holy shit," the girl in front of me yelled.

"This was my favorite shirt."

"Watch your language," her mother said. She touched the fine sprinkle of makeup on the sleeve of her white jacket tentatively with one finger. "I hope you're effing insured," she added in my direction.

I wiped some dribbles off my cheek with the back of my hand and turned to look at Sean Ryan. He was covered.

"Sorry about that," he said. His eyes were scrunched shut, and he was holding his palms up, like he was waiting for a miracle.

Mario started making dry cleaning arrangements with the worst case scenarios and passing out wipes. I reached out and grabbed two. I handed one to Sean Ryan.

"Thanks," he said. He spread the wipe over his hands and leaned forward and buried his face in it. "A buddy of mine is covering for me so I can take a break," he mumbled into his hands. "I was about to ask you if you wanted to join me."

Sure, he was kind of sweet and funny now. They were always nice to you in the beginning. Then, before you knew it, your life was exploding all over the place, with little jagged pieces of your heart flying everywhere.

I waited until he lifted his head up again. "Does it look like I can take a break?" I asked before I went on to the next face.

Four hours and seven packs of triangular sponges later, I was so sick of airbrushing I could have turned the gun on myself. To make matters worse, since I'd been the last to arrive, everybody else just did the bare minimum for cleanup and waltzed right out of there. That meant I had to stay to help Mario pack up our stuff and lug it out.

To possibly speed up the payment process, Mario headed off to see if he could hand deliver the invoice to someone. I curled up in one of the hydraulic chairs and closed my eyes, waiting for a second wind.

"Whew. That bad, huh?" I heard Sean Ryan's voice say from a distance.

I opened my eyes, then closed them again. "Haven't you done enough already?" I asked.

"I said I was sorry. Is it safe to come over? I mean, are you unarmed now?"

"Cute," I said. I kept my eyes closed. As far as men were concerned, my philosophy was thoroughly worked out: Been There, Done That, Who Needs Them.

I finally opened my eyes, just out of idle curiosity. Sean Ryan was looking down at me. My eyes met his, and I felt a jolt that seriously conflicted with my philosophy. I ignored it.

I focused instead on the two dots of foundation on his right eyebrow. They weren't even his shade. He had one of his boxes tucked under his arm like a football.

"What is that anyway?" I asked. "They sure were selling like hotcakes." I swung my legs around so they touched the floor and pushed myself up a little.

He smiled his lopsided smile. "A kit. For writing your college application essays." He held it out to me.

I crossed my arms over my chest. "What do you mean, a kit?"

"You know, cards with essay starters, a questionnaire to isolate your best shot personal topic to sell yourself to the college of your dreams, inspirational stories from kids who've lived through it and are now happily ensconced at their first-choice college, a note to parents about backing off, some caffeine product samples, a cattle prod. An old friend of mine who's a high school guidance counselor came up with the idea. I helped him put it together, and now I'm test marketing it for him."

I looked up at him. "A cattle prod?"

He held out the box again. "Go ahead, look. I wouldn't joke around about something like that."

"Right," I said. "Nice box," I added. It was kind of abstract and hip. Instead of a picture of some kiss-up straight-A student on the cover, it had a skull and crossbones and COLLEGE APPLICATION SURVIVAL KIT printed in bright red letters.

"Thanks," he said. "It's getting a great response."

I could just see Mario working his way back over. I dragged myself up to a standing position. "Well, good luck with it," I said.

Sean Ryan reached into his jacket pocket. He held one of his cards out to me. "You know, I was thinking. Maybe you should put together a makeup kit."

"Oh, boy," I said. "Now I get it. Is this like a pyramid scheme or something?"

"What are you talking about?"

"You know, you only make money on your kit if you bring in enough other kit makers?"

He shook his head and started putting the card back in his pocket. "Never mind," he said. He looked up. "What is your problem anyway?"

"How much time do you have?"

Mario came back and started folding the tables. I took a step in his direction. "Listen," I said. "Maybe you should find someone else to try your kit line on. Nothing

38

personal, but I'm completely over men."

He nodded his head calmly, as if nothing I could ever say to him would shock him. "Since when?" he asked.

"Since. My. Half. Sister. Started. Dating. My. Husband."

That got him. He opened his eyes wide, despite himself. "Ouch. That'd do it. Whew."

"Yeah, well."

He held out the card again. "Here, take this anyway. Just in case you change your mind."

I looked at him. He looked at me. He tilted his head. I tilted mine. I had a sudden stupid urge to toss my hair, run my tongue along my lower lip to make it shine, say something flirty. Instead I straightened my head back out and took a step away.

"About the kit," he said. He leaned over and put the card in my case.

I blew out a puff of air. "You'd probably turn out to be a homicidal maniac."

He smiled. "Maybe. But, who knows, I might be a really nice guy."

4

I was just finishing up Esther Williams. Her name was really Esther Williamson, but she'd shortened it to sound more glamorous after she "dumped that last clown I married." She had broad shoulders and narrow hips, and she liked to tell people she was the famous swimmer from the movies. She said she got a lot of dates that way.

This Esther Williams was well into her eighties. She came into Salon de Lucio at least once a week for a wash and set, something we didn't even have a price for anymore. We gave her a special deal because she was a regular, and also because she had a manicure every week, a pedicure every other week, and a full makeup complete with false eyelashes every time she came in. At least one of those clowns must have left her some serious money.

She also paid less because Salon de Lucio was our flagship salon. It was separated from the house my father lived in by only a breezeway, so it had the cheapest prices of any of my father's salons. The way he looked at it, the greater the distance he had to travel to get there, the more he should charge. Even Mario couldn't talk him out of that one.

Today, Esther Williams was getting her monthly color done, too. She liked to sit with her Clairol Professional 37D Iced Brown on for a full four hours, something I'd never put up with from any other client. She brought her portable DVD player and yoga mat with her, and after I applied her color, she'd go off to the kiddie area.

The kiddie area was in the back corner of the room, and my siblings and I had all practically grown up there. It was really just a slightly raised platform, partitioned off by a short Tuscan-style fake stone wall and a wrought iron baby gate. My avocado green Easy-Bake oven was still in there.

Esther Williams would unroll her mat on the matching avocado green shag rug and plop the DVD player down on the wall. She'd exercise along with a DVD — sometimes yoga, sometimes tai chi, sometimes *Solo Salsa with Sizzle.* Then she'd watch an Esther Williams movie, maybe *Million Dollar Mermaid* or *Dangerous When Wet.* After that, she'd flip through a magazine or take a nap. If any kids showed up, they'd just play around her. It wasn't like she got in anyone's way.

Four hours was a long time for a hair color. In fact it was eight times longer than the Clairol professional directions recommended. But about three or four years ago, I'd just finished brushing on Esther Williams's color. I covered her hair in a clear plastic cap to build up the heat and accelerate the color. I tucked cotton under the elastic to absorb any drips. She made a funny sound.

"I don't feel so good," she said. She had one hand up by her shoulder, like she was pledging allegiance.

She didn't look so good either. She was having a hard time catching her breath, and she was all fluttery and anxious. I called 911 and went back to hold her hand until the ambulance came.

While we waited, I thought hard about rinsing off her color. On the one hand, I didn't want to be responsible for killing her. On the other hand, Esther Williams was a tough cookie. If she made it, I knew she'd be the one to kill me if her hair fell out.

In the end, I was afraid to risk a rinse. I followed her out to the ambulance, then got back to work. Four hours later, a cruiser pulled up and a cop walked Esther back into the shop. He waited while I rinsed off her color and styled her hair, then drove her home. She said it was the best damn dye job she ever had. And so now she always sat for exactly four hours.

I took the last pink plastic roller out of Esther Williams's hair and started teasing it with a rattail comb. After I got her the volume she liked, I gave her enough aerosol spray to last her for at least a week.

"You're gorgeous," I said when I finished.

"What else is new?" she said. "Okay, now give me some eyes."

I gave her some eyes, smoky eyes at that. Almay color cream eye shadow in Mocha Shimmer, Bobbi Brown long-wear gel eyeliner in Black Ink, and NYC eyelashes. They were self-adhesive, but I added some extra glue anyway, just to make sure she didn't lose one before I saw her again. Next came lots of Maybelline Great Lash mascara in Very Black. Then I gave her some lips with Max Factor Lipfinity in Passionate.

"Now go get Lucky," Esther Williams said.

My father had been trying to get people to call him Lucio since he'd opened this salon thirty-five years ago. But he was still Lucky Larry Shaughnessy to almost everyone in Marshbury, Massachusetts.

"Sorry," I said the way he always told me to. "He's off getting ready for the staff meeting." The truth was he was tiptoeing around, hiding from Esther Williams.

"Handsome hunka burning man, that dad of yours. Don't let anyone tell you different. What's he need meetings for? He could sell this place for a million bucks and retire until his next life started up."

The parking lot alone was probably worth a million bucks. My father's raised ranch, with the Italianate columns, two-tiered fountain, and attached salon he'd added, overlooked Marshbury harbor. It was just about the only waterfront property on the street that hadn't been ripped down for midrise condos with street-level shops. Even though the house and salon had been there the longest, they looked more like intruders with every passing year.

"Yeah," I said. "But then who would he boss around?"

"Me." Esther Williams put her glasses back on and leaned into the mirror for a closer look. "I keep telling him. He should try an older woman once before he dies."

The Friday staff meeting was our family's version of Sunday dinner. As soon as we closed the salon and everybody got there, my father called in the pizza order. That gave us about twenty minutes to tend to business before the food arrived.

Even if you weren't related, you stayed for at least a slice of pizza. And sometimes the stylists who weren't working arrived early, so they could experiment. Two of the newest stylists had been there for about an hour already today, practicing updos on each other. Now they both looked like they needed to find a prom fast.

"*Woilà,*" one of them said, pinning down the other's final curl with a bobby pin.

Mario and I looked at each other. "*Woilà?*" we both mouthed.

My father came in through the breezeway door, wearing a long white tunic over bell-bottom jeans. This is a challenging look for a man to pull off, especially one over seventy, but he managed. He was flipping through the day's mail, separating the letters from Realtors and developers from the pack. "Barracudas," he said. "They're all a bunch of barracudas." He crumpled up the unopened letters and threw them into the wastebasket behind the reception counter.

He put the rest of the mail down on the counter and started snapping his fingers, alternating hands the way beatniks did when they heard a good poem in the '60s. "Hear ye, hear ye," my father said. "The court's in session and here comes da judge."

This was our signal to arrange our chairs in a semicircle around him. I put mine down as far away from Sophia's as I could get. My father stopped snapping so he could finger the *cornicello* that hung from a thick gold chain around his neck. It was made out of bright red coral capped in a gold crown, and it was shaped like a horn. Maybe if we were really Italian I'd know whether *cornicello* was actually even the word for horn.

I knew there were pedophiles and bibliophiles, even Francophiles. But my father was the only Italiophile I'd ever met. I thought it might be partly the businessman in him: an Italian hair salon just sounded way more glamorous than an Irish one would. I mean, how much money could you really charge at Salon de Seamus, especially if you lived in the part of Massachusetts everybody called the Irish Riviera? But he'd also spent his very first honeymoon with his very first wife in a borrowed house in Tuscany. The Lucky Larry Shaughnessy and Mary Margaret O'Neill Italy Experience had had an irrevocable impact on him, not to mention the first names of all his future children.

"Any more wedding news?" Angela asked Mario.

Mario turned to Todd. Todd was Mario's husband, our accountant-slash-business manager, and along with Mario, one of the two fathers of Andrew, my nephew and the groom-to-be. Ours was not an uncomplicated family.

They both shook their heads. "Just that Amy's parents are driving them crazy," Mario said. "They wanted a simple wedding, but things are getting more out of control every day. Apparently they like to do it up big in Atlanta. I still can't believe they're having it at the Margaret Mitchell House."

"Will you get to watch *Gone With the Wind*?" one of the stylists asked.

"Yeah," I said. "I think it's right before the vows."

"Tell me again," my father said. "Are the bride's parents queer, too?"

"Of course they are," Mario said, even though they were really just Southern. "By the way, Dad, Donald Trump called. He said he wants his hair back."

There were lots of unusual things about our family, not the least of which was our father's hair. It was actually darker than The

47

Donald's and painstakingly styled by my father. Every morning he started with a handful of thickening mousse. Then he pulled it strand by strand across the top of his head. Finally, he filled in with a spray designed to "Cover Your Bald Spot Instantly." Maybe his shiny brown eyes and the swagger in his step took your attention away from the fake hair on his scalp, since he'd still managed to attract three ex-wives.

"Is Mom going to the wedding?" Angela asked.

I held my breath, the way I always did when my mother was mentioned in front of my father.

"She's the grandmother. Of course she is," Mario said. "At least I think she is."

My father grabbed his *cornicello.* He really believed it warded off the evil eye. "Okay, that's enough," he said. "Back to business."

Tulia pushed the front door open. Her three kids came running in to hug their grandfather around the knees. Mack was wearing a red T-shirt over his bathing suit and carried a red toy train. Maggie and her doll were both dressed in blue sundresses. Myles and the wagon he was pulling were both yellow. I leaned over and whispered to Mario, "Is she actually color-coding her kids, do you think?"

"Maybe. I'm surprised Dad didn't try that with us, he's such a control freak. I'd be the one in therapy, saying, 'It all started because everybody but me got to be a primary color.'"

Todd laughed, and he and Mario exchanged one of those married looks I vaguely remembered. "It would make a great memoir," Todd said. "*I Was a Secondary Color: A Shocking Story of Sibling Abuse.*"

Tulia's mother came in right behind her and headed for a chair. "Sorry," Tulia said. "Mike had to work late, and I forgot it was Mom's week for the meeting."

"No skin off my nose," my father said. "They'll be working here soon enough anyway." He peeled the kids off him, and they headed over to the kiddie area.

When people first meet us as a group, we probably should give them a diagram. Even then they might not be able to get us all straight. It's just the way it is with big, messy families. I tell everybody to take notes — there might be a test later.

It didn't help that we all looked so much alike. My father's children all had thick brown hair and pale skin, plus big eyes and, most of the time, big smiles. His ex-wives looked pretty much the same, except for the hair, which ran the gamut from gray to gold.

Sometimes when I was explaining my family to people, I'd call my father's ex-wives A, B, and C to simplify things. Mary, who was Angela's, Mario's, and my mother, was A. Tulia's mother, Didi, was B. Linda, who was Sophia's mother, was C. It also simplified things that, after a rocky transition from B to C that included some minor hair pulling, Didi and Linda worked in separate salons and went to the weekly meeting on alternate Fridays. My mother didn't go at all. She lived a few towns away and had gone back to school to become a social worker as soon as she left my father, which was shortly after he started fooling around with Didi, his second wife-to-be.

My father was looking particularly dapper these days. This probably meant his fourth ex-wife-to-be was somewhere in the wings. I just hoped if she ended up working for us, she at least knew how to give a decent haircut.

"Now where were we?" my father asked.

"Nowhere yet," I said.

"Angela," my father said. "Sophia. I mean Bella. You're a beautiful girl, but you have to learn to watch the big *bocca* talk."

"That would be mouth," Mario whispered.

I elbowed him.

"How're we doing in the moolah department, Toddy?" my father asked.

"Not bad, Lucky, not bad at all," Todd said. When it came to handling his father-in-law's political incorrectness and annoying nicknames, he'd come a long way. "We've got most clients booking their next appointment before they leave the salons. We could use some more action in product sales though."

"People don't want to pay the prices," Angela said. "*Project Runway* killed us. I mean, how do you convince people that Aveda hairspray is worth the money, when they were on TV raving about a two-dollar can of Finesse Très Two?"

"I don't know," I said. "It can work both ways. Everybody knows Maybelline Great Lash is the best mascara, but I spray paint the outside gold before I put it in my case, so my clients think I'm using all high-end products."

"Do you really?" Mario asked. "I didn't know that. That's a great idea."

I struck a pose. "Lots more where that came from," I said.

"Yeah, right," Angela said.

"Bella knows everything," Tulia said. "Hasn't she told you yet?"

"Sure she does," Angela said. "She even

managed to airbrush an entire crowd at once this week."

I wondered if all big families who traveled in a pack turned on their own like this. I knew enough to wait it out and not rise to the bait. Eventually they'd start picking on somebody else. I probably would even have kept my big *bocca* shut, except I caught a glimpse of Sophia. I really wanted to wipe that smirk off her face.

"Well," I said. "I know enough. In fact, someone approached me this week to see if I wanted to create a makeup kit." I reached for details. "You know, to be sold."

"You mean that guy hitting on you at the college fair?" Mario asked.

"If anybody does a kit, my Tulia should do a kit," Tulia's mother, Didi, said.

"He was so not hitting on me," I said. "He just thought I was talented."

"Sure he did," Angela said.

"That's not a bad idea," Todd said. "I bet we could get the companies to kick in some product samples. I mean, why not, it would be free advertising for them. They might even pay for placement."

"What if we added recipes?" Angela asked. "You know, spa cuisine?"

My father was snapping his fingers again. "I'm loving this," he said. "The Salon de

Lucio Beauty Kit. All soft and Romany, maybe tied up like a toga. When they open the box, it'll be like they died and went to Italy."

I cleared my throat. "Excuse me?" I said.

"Sophia can add something about celebrity makeup, since she's got all the high-profile clients," my traitor brother Mario actually said.

"Bath salts and massage oils would be good, too," Tulia said. "And I love that gel that turns hot when you rub your hands together."

I jumped up, since nobody seemed to be hearing me. "Hello-oh," I said.

"I have a great recipe for lemon mayonnaise. You can use it for a hair mask. Or eat it, obviously," Angela said.

"Stop," I yelled. "Stop, stop, stop. Stop."

Everybody stopped.

"I'm sick and tired of everyone taking everything away from me," I heard myself saying. "It's *my* beauty kit. It's *my* life. It's *my* . . ." — I looked right at Sophia — ". . . husband," I said.

And then I ran out.

5

The tears I was fighting dried right up as soon as I saw Craig in the parking lot.

Craig started up his Lexus as soon as he saw me coming.

I bent down and picked up a rock.

In his haste to get out of the salon parking lot, my ex-husband burned some serious rubber. That couldn't possibly be good for his little leased tires.

"Go lease a brain," I yelled after him. Finding my inner bully was surprisingly exhilarating, so I threw the rock at his car. It bounced off his rear license plate with a satisfying clunk. I brushed my hands off and headed for my own car. The sign in the front window of the salon mocked me: SUMMER BLOWOUT. Ha.

"They're not your kids, Bella," I said to my rearview mirror. "Forget about them."

I pulled out of the parking lot and took a right. I'd been repeating this over and over to myself like a bad mantra ever since Craig had said it.

It was the thing that really got to me. I mean, I'd written off Sophia. I'd written off Craig. But I wasn't sure I'd ever forget about the kids. For almost ten years I'd spent Wednesday nights and every other weekend with Craig's kids. And every other holiday and every other school vacation and half the summer. I'd caught colds from them and helped them with their homework. Craig and I had taken them on almost all our vacations. We'd decided not to have kids of our own pretty much because of them. Actually, almost completely because of them. Neither of us thought it was fair the way fathers just moved on to the next set of kids.

At least my father had never done that. He'd just rolled us all into his next family. Except my mother, who was the only one who'd resisted, who'd carved out a new life of her own. But, idiot that I was, I'd gone along with Craig. I'd even managed to convince myself that Luke and Lizzie were essentially my kids, too.

Ha. They'd blown me off completely as soon as their father dumped me. Luke had another year of college left, and Lizzie would be heading off to her freshman year soon. I could have helped her pick out things for her dorm room. I had much better taste than her real mother. I could have helped her shop for clothes. And makeup. Lizzie's hair was probably a mess by now. Anybody could be cutting it.

Wait. Sophia was probably cutting Lizzie's hair. I put on my blinker and pulled over to the side of the road. Sophia was cutting Lizzie's hair.

I just sat there, on the side of the street, for a while. Maybe five seconds, maybe five minutes, maybe an hour. I didn't bother to notice, because it didn't really matter. I mean, it's not like anyone would have missed me.

I knew I needed to get a grip. Wallowing like this was not my nature. I was strong. I was confident. All my life you could practically hear me roar. I wasn't even all that freaked out when, a little over a year ago, my husband of ten years packed his bags and told me he needed some space.

There was a part of me that was relieved I didn't have to be the one to say it. We'd been drifting apart for a while, making lots of snide remarks, just not really liking each other much anymore. I thought some of it might have to do with Lizzie getting ready to graduate from high school. Craig's kids had preexisted our relationship, so they'd always been part of the deal. Now we'd have to figure out what, if anything, we were without them.

Looking back, it was odd that Sophia started spending more time with me then, not less. You'd think I'd be the last person on earth she'd want to be around once she'd set her sights on my husband. But in the months both before and after Craig moved out, she stopped by and she called. A lot. Maybe if she couldn't be with him openly yet, the next best thing was being with the person who was still technically married to him.

And that's how I found out. Craig had been gone for less than a month. Sophia and I were out shopping together. I stayed in the car while she ran in to pick up some dry cleaning. Her cell phone rang. I picked it up without thinking and said hello.

It was Craig. I guess he wasn't expecting me to answer, and Sophia and I had always sounded a lot alike. "So, are we on for tonight?" he asked.

"Not if I can help it," I said. And I hung up.

"How could you?" I asked when Sophia came back to the car.

"What?" she said.

"That was Craig." My heart was beating like a maniac. I could hear blood pounding in my ears, and I wondered if Sophia could, too.

She reached back and hooked the hangers over the handle in the backseat of her car, then turned around and put both hands on the steering wheel. She didn't look at me. "No it wasn't," she said. "It must have been someone else."

I looked straight ahead. I reached into my bag and pulled out a lipstick, a sheer muted grape called Damage, and put it on in quick, ruthless strokes. "He told me," I lied. "He said you've slept together at least twelve times."

"We have not," she said. "It was only —"

"Ha," I said. I smacked my lips to blend the color. "Gotcha."

They'd both sworn up and down that nothing had happened until after Craig and I had split up. Oh, puh-lease. And it didn't really even matter. A sister is still a sister, even if she's a half sister, and a husband is still off limits to everyone who loves you, even if he's on his way to becoming an ex. I thought these were basic rules everybody followed.

Mario got me the name of a lawyer, and I called the next day. Massachusetts allows no-fault divorce based on irreconcilable breakdown of the marriage. There were no kids or property acquired during our marriage. So it was no fuss, no muss. A 120-day waiting period, plus about four more months, and I had my divorce papers. Piece of cake.

I rolled down the windows and took a deep breath, hoping it might make me feel better. No such luck. Air was highly overrated. I pushed the lever that released my trunk. I opened my car door and jumped out. A car swerved around me, and the guy driving it leaned on his horn. I gave him the finger.

I lifted the hood of the trunk and reached in and opened my case. It was starting to get dark already, so I had to root around to find Sean Ryan's card.

I'd been hanging around acting like a victim long enough, and a makeup kit seemed like it might be my best shot at some forward motion. Especially since, at the moment, it was the only thing I could think of.

"Hi," Sean Ryan's voice said. Actually, according to his card, Sean was his first name and Ryan his last. But it was too late for that. He'd already become Sean Ryan in my mind.

"Hi," I said. I felt that quick flash of relief I get when something happens so easily it's clearly meant to be.

"You've reached me, but I'm either off hang gliding in Argentina, or I'm not answering the phone. So leave a message."

I hung up without leaving a message. Why even bother. Sean Ryan was a man. Men sucked. Therefore, by definition, Sean Ryan would ultimately suck, too. All I really wanted from him was to find out how to make a kit of my own, and with my luck, he would probably turn out to be some kind of scam artist anyway.

I was still parked on the side of the road, and I was leaning back against my car, a red Volkswagen bug with a black convertible top. Since I had dark brown hair and green eyes, I looked great in that car. People don't think about that enough, in my opinion. Why buy a car in a color that doesn't work on you? There's nothing worse than seeing an otherwise attractive woman driving by in a drab gray car that saps the color right out of her face.

Not that the right car seemed to be doing me much good at the moment, but I climbed back in anyway. I sat there until every single car coming at me had turned on its headlights. Then I sat there some more, until the flash of each passing light really started getting on my nerves.

Finally, I started driving. Up and down the streets of Marshbury, going really slow so I could look inside the windows I passed. It was amazing how many people didn't bother with their blinds. They just left their houses opened up like great big fishbowls. I passed people watching TV, people eating dinner, even one couple making out in an upstairs window. They were really going at it. They'd probably just met. They might think they had it all going on now, but just wait. Pretty soon they'd be driving around by themselves, too.

Okay, before I turned into a certifiable Peeping Tom, I had to find something else to do. I really didn't want to go home and face all the worried messages everyone had probably left for me. Mario, for sure. And most likely Angela and my father. Possibly one of the stylists. And maybe even Tulia, though she was pretty self-absorbed. I didn't usually fall apart that way in front of people. I wasn't the one who ran out of a room. I was the one who made the other person run.

When we were first together, I used to think Craig and I were like complementary colors. I was orange and he was blue, or maybe I was red and he was green. In any case, we each made the other stand out. Because I was opinionated, Craig appeared even more laid-back. Craig thought first, then acted. I acted and reacted immediately. In the early years, our differences created both excitement and balance. But when we started to drift apart, it was as if we didn't even speak the same language. The more he detached, the more I pushed. The more I pushed, the more he detached. We were still exactly the same people, except somehow now our colors clashed.

Before I ran out of gas, I had to find somewhere to go. I tried to think of a friend who might be home on a Friday night, someone who might not have anything to do tonight either. Most of Craig's and my friends had been couples friends. I'd always been independent, but I was flattered that Craig wanted to be with me all the time. He had enough of a problem with me spending so much time with my family, so I kind of let my female friendships slide while I was married. I hadn't quite had the energy yet to figure out how to start rekindling those. Do you just show up one day and say, *Hi, I'm ba-ack?*

I was probably halfway there before I realized I was driving to my mother's house.

As much as I loved my mother, this was a sad way to spend a Friday night on so many levels. First and foremost was that sympathy was not my mother's strong suit.

I turned off the main drag into my mother's gated townhouse complex. I'd never seen anyone in the guardhouse in the two years since she'd moved there, so I really didn't know what that was all about. Maybe they kept meaning to get a guard, like I kept meaning to get on with my life. Maybe by the time they got a guard, I'd be ready to date him.

The buildings all looked pretty much the same from the outside, and I always forgot whether my mother lived in Building B or D. I pulled into the Building C parking lot, so I wouldn't have to drag myself too far if I guessed wrong the first time. As soon as I got out of the car, I remembered it was Building B. Definitely. I'd have to write it on my hand so I'd remember next time.

Inside the tiny lobby, I pushed the buzzer marked M. O'NEILL. I waited. My stomach growled. I pushed it again. Great. Even my mother had a life. I slid down to the floor of the lobby and called her cell phone.

"Hi there," her voice said after the fourth ring. "I'm either out saving the world or just plain having too much fun to answer my phone. So please leave a message at the tone."

I hung up. What was the telephone world coming to? Was I the only one who still had my default greeting? I applied some Chap-Stick Medicated Classic to my parched lips. I looked at my phone for a long moment, then dialed my voice mail. I punched in my password, then pressed three to change my personal options. Then I pressed one to change my greeting. I was thoroughly exhausted from all that effort, but I somehow managed to record a new message.

"Hi, I'm either off skinny-dipping in Corsica with my hot new boyfriend, or out screwing my ex-husband's brother. But, hey, feel free to leave me a message anyway."

Then I checked my messages so I wouldn't have to do it later.

Not a one.

6

The ring of the phone woke me up from a dead, depressed sleep. I rolled over an empty container of ice cream on my way to answer it. A chocolate-swirled puddle leached out from the crushed container and onto my pillowcase. I circled my finger around in it and licked it off. My standards must really be slipping if I'd left that much in there.

"What," I said when I found my phone.

"Hey," Mario's voice said. "Don't take it out on me. I'm just calling to make sure you remember you've got a wedding. Hair and makeup for the whole bridal party at nine. Bride, mother of bride, matron of honor, three bridesmaids. The wedding starts at two, so don't be late."

I kicked my way out of the covers. "You know, a little sympathy would go a long way."

Mario paused, never a good sign. "Sophia

was really upset," he said finally. "I'm worried about her."

"Excuse me?" I said.

"You were a little rough on her, don't you think?"

I shut my eyes. "Ohmigod. Is everyone else taking her side, too?"

"We're just trying to see both sides, Bella. You and Craig *were* already separated when they started dating."

"Oh, stop. Everybody always says that." I pushed myself out of bed and started aiming for the coffeemaker. "We have no idea how long it was really going on. I mean, why else would Craig have left me?"

"Bottom line, you should feel lucky. Craig's an idiot."

Of course, I was out of coffee filters. I pulled off a hunk of paper towel from the roll and tried to fold it into a cone. "So what," I said. "He was *my* idiot."

I opened my freezer and grabbed the coffee and started shaking it on top of the paper towel. Then I added tap water and pushed the On button.

I opened the refrigerator next and grabbed a tube of Sephora Fresh Gloss, which had a clean, minty scent that worked well with my toothpaste. I was amazed at how many women didn't know enough to keep their lip gloss in the refrigerator. Not only does it keep it from melting in the summer, but it lasts longer that way.

The cool sensation on my lips was almost enough to make me feel human again. A quick fix in a life where there are no others.

I traded the lip gloss for a yogurt and managed to find a clean spoon.

"Love happens, Bella," Mario said into the phone that was still attached to my ear.

"*Love happens?* What kind of bullshit is that?"

I took a spoonful of yogurt, then spit it into the sink and rinsed out my mouth. Belatedly, I looked for the expiration date, which was covered with a price sticker. Why did everything always have to be so complicated?

"Bella?"

I poured some coffee and took a gulp to get rid of the sour yogurt taste. "Yeah, I'm here. It's the Harborside Inn, right? What's the bridal party's name?"

"Right, the Harborside. They've got the wedding suite. I'm not sure about the name. The bride's father came by the salon. Twice. The first time he said it, it sounded like Psilocybin, and the second time like Silly Siren. But he paid for everything up front, in cash no less, so we're good to go."

"Silly Siren?"

If the bride didn't stop dry heaving, I was seriously going to burn her with the curling iron. Of course, this might be her best shot at being a hot bride. She had baby fine hair and a fishlike mouth, and the cords of her neck stuck out every time she started up again.

"She always does this," one of her bridesmaids said. "You should have seen her before the engagement party."

I'd already finished doing airbrush makeup and hair on the matron of honor, who looked like an older version of the bride, minus the dry heaves, as well as the three bridesmaids. Now they were throwing things all over the bridal suite and getting dressed in cornflower blue tea-length taffeta bubble dresses with shirred bodices and empire waists that didn't do much for any of their body types.

Normally, I would have done the mother of the bride next, but she was huddled in a corner, and she waved me off when I approached her. So I figured I'd get the bride out of the way and then go back to her.

As if things weren't crazy enough, there were two wild little kids in shorts and striped polo shirts running around screaming. And on top of that, a tiny yippy dog kept nipping around my ankles. The dog was also wearing a cornflower blue taffeta bubble dress, but it was cut a bit shorter than tea length — probably so the tiny yipper wouldn't pee on it — and pinned in the back with a sparkly brooch.

"Is this hotel pet friendly?" I asked. We'd never had dogs growing up, and I still hadn't quite managed to grasp the point of them.

"Stop being so high maintenance, Precious," the bride said between bouts. "Next time I am so getting a Peekapoo."

Precious ignored her and kept nipping at the air around my ankles. The bride picked her up and threw her on one of the beds. No wonder the poor dog had no manners.

The bride's father had been pacing in the hallway when I'd stepped off the elevator and headed for the bridal suite. He was tall and old-fashioned-looking, with wavy gray hair slathered with hair pomade. He had the oddest accent, and he introduced himself as Mr. Something or Other without shaking my hand. Mario was right. It could have been either Psilocybin or Silly Siren. Or even Silver Sighting.

Now he pushed the door to the bridal suite open. He averted his eyes, walked in far enough to hand the bride a cell phone, then turned around and walked back out again. This was probably a good thing, since two of the bridesmaids were in the process of exchanging bras.

"This is amazing," one of them said. "Your B bra pushes up my C cleavage."

"And your C bra," the other one said, "makes my A cleavage look like there's something there."

I was about to call Maidenform to sign them up for a commercial, when the bride closed the cell phone. She really started dry heaving in earnest now. I was never going to get rid of this wedding party if I didn't get her under control.

"Go get some wine," I whispered to the only bridesmaid left wearing her own bra. "Fast."

Then I turned on the TV to the Food Network. Even the wild little kids and the tiny yippy dog settled down. We all sat there and watched for a few moments, and I tried to learn about blanching, which was something I'd never fully understood either.

"That was John," the bride said between heaves. "He's the groom. He couldn't get me on my cell. I must have left it on vibrate."

"Shh," I said. "Wait." Precious came over

and yipped and circled a few times, then peed on the rug. I was right about the dress. It stayed dry as a bone.

The wild little kids screamed. They ran over to take a closer look at the pee. Precious jumped back up on the bed without being thrown. The mother of the bride dropped a towel on top of the pee and stepped on it, which made the wild little kids scream some more.

The bridesmaid returned from the bar with an open bottle of white wine. She poured a glass, and the bride gulped it down.

"They have to go back to Braintree," she said when she finished. "They got all the way back with the tuxes, and they forgot to give them any pants."

"Ooh," I said. "I like it. A *Risky Business* kind of wedding. You know, tux jackets with the shirttails sticking out, and all those sexy male legs."

The bride started to giggle. I grabbed a hunk of hair and got going on the rest of her corkscrew curls with the curling iron

"Maybe we could find them some kilts and a bagpipe," the C cup bridesmaid said. The bridesmaid with the wine handed her the bottle, and she took a big slug and handed it back.

"They're going to stop by the walk-in clinic and get a throat culture while they're up there. John thinks he might have strep throat."

"He's a total hypochondriac," the A cup bridesmaid said.

"Guess who's having a baby?" the bridesmaid in her own bra said. "Allison and Mark."

"Are they back together?"

"They were for one night. Don't tell her I told you."

I got the last curl nailed down without any hitches. That wine was really working. Now all I had left was the mother of the bride, who got up and went to the bathroom as soon as she saw I was ready for her.

"What's her problem?" I asked the matron of honor.

The matron of honor shrugged. "She's still not over my wedding. She thinks one of the makeup people insulted her."

The bathroom door opened. "I heard her say it," the mother of the bride said. "She said, 'I don't do old eyes.'"

"No she didn't," the matron of honor said. "She said to the other one, 'Why don't you do her. You're better at older eyes.'"

"Same thing," the mother of the bride said.

"It is not, Mom," the matron of honor said. "Not even close."

I patted the stool in front of me. "Sit," I said. "I'll give you eyes so young the bartender will have to ask for your ID."

Like many women her age, the mother of the bride was the victim of serious eyebrow overplucking. I gave her a few drops of Visine, primed her, dabbed some concealer around her eyes and nose, and airbrushed her. Then I filled out her eyebrows with an angled brush and soft brown eyebrow powder and told her never, ever to use an eyebrow pencil on them again.

I handed her my eyelash curler and let her do that part herself. I'd learned this the hard way when one of my clients sneezed while I was curling her eyelashes. I still cringed when I thought about that one. But curled eyelashes really make eyes of any age pop, so it was worth waiting for her to figure it out.

Then I gave her smoky eyes, and to minimize her droopy eyelids, I added a bit of deeper brown on the saggy parts. Next I added some frosty white under her brows. If you're careful not to overdo it, just a bit of frosted eye shadow there can really open up your eyes and make you look younger. I added some subtle false eyelashes and lots of Maybelline Intense XXL mascara in brownish black. I finished her off with Red Hot Mama lips.

"Give some extra money to the girl," the mother of the bride said when the father walked in again. He reached into his pocket and handed me some pretty big bills, so I decided not to be too insulted.

My work here was done. Often the photographer showed up to stage some fully made-up shots of the wedding party pretending to get ready, but at least I'd been spared that one today. They must have decided to meet the photographer at the wedding. I started packing up my case. The matron of honor hung up her phone, then walked over and looked out the window. She whispered something to her father and blew a kiss in the direction of the wild little kids.

The bride picked up Precious and tucked her under one arm. One of the bridesmaids offered her the bottle of wine. She grabbed it with her free hand and took another long gulp. The bride's mother smiled at herself in the mirror over the bed and started heading for the door, and the bridesmaids followed.

The father of the bride reached into his pocket and pulled out his wad of bills again. He peeled off some good ones and handed them to me.

It sounded like he said, "The babysitter will be here in a minute." But it also might have been, "The lady slipper will steer in a cynic."

Either way, before I knew what hit me, the wild little kids and I were alone.

7

"Call social services," my mother said. "Wait, I'll get you the number for the Child-at-Risk Hotline."

I'd gone into the bedroom to make the phone call to my mother. I stuck my head back into the living room to peek at the kids. They were kind of cute when they quieted down. They were both sucking their thumbs while they learned to make Simple Stovetop Mocha Pudding. Watching the chocolate melt in the double boiler was pretty mesmerizing in high definition, and it was also interesting to note that you should always turn off the heat *before* you stir in the vanilla. Craig's kids had loved to cook at that age.

"Bella," my mother's voice said in my ear. "Are you still there?"

"Oh, sorry," I said. "I don't know. If I did that, they'd probably want some of the money back."

"You took money to watch them?"

"Well," I said. "It's not like I had much of a choice."

"Bella," my mother said. "Did you or did you not find two abandoned children?"

My mother was such a social worker sometimes. "Never mind," I said. "So, what else is new? Where were you last night?"

"Out with a friend," my mother said. "So, do we or do we not have a crisis here?"

I walked over to the bar area. There was a nice, big fruit basket, so I helped myself to an apple. "Not," I said.

"Okay then. Wait, I have another call coming in. Listen, I'll give you a call later, okay? Love you."

"Love you, too," I said to dead air. I closed my phone. I sat on the edge of the bed and looked out the window. I ate my apple. The bridal suite had a great view of Marshbury harbor. It looked like everybody with a boat was heading out to enjoy this perfect late August day.

I finished the apple and checked the clock radio beside the couch. The bride was probably walking down the aisle right about now. With luck, the wine hadn't worn off yet, since it would be a shame to start dry heaving on the altar. I wondered if the groom really had strep throat. I wondered if he was wearing pants.

I could feel myself just about to start strolling down memory lane to the foggy past of *my* wedding. I definitely didn't want to go there, so I took a deep breath and shook it off. I looked out the window again, hoping to see some sign of the babysitter, not that I had any idea what she, or even he, might look like.

The cooking show must have gone to a commercial, because the wild little kids ran into the room and started jumping on the bed and screaming at the top of their lungs. Still, no one banged on the door or called to complain. The bridal suite must be practically soundproof. I wondered if they advertised it that way.

All that yelling was starting to give me a headache. I did some quick math and decided I'd stayed here long enough to have earned the extra cash.

"Hey," I said. "How about some makeup before we hit the road?"

The wild little kids were buckled in the back of my Volkswagen bug, and I was driving really slowly, since I was pretty sure that technically they should still have been riding in car seats.

I took a look at them in the rearview mirror. They weren't exactly fit for a wedding reception in those striped polo shirts, but at least the makeup dressed them up a bit. They'd both giggled a lot when I airbrushed them, especially the little boy. I'd gone easy on the rest of the makeup though, so they wouldn't turn out looking like those awful little beauty pageant kids.

I took a left at the end of Front Street. The tricky part was that I didn't actually know where the reception was. This might have been problematic in a town bigger than Marshbury, but there were only three possibilities, so I knew we'd find it eventually. Unless, of course, they'd gone out of town, but I wasn't going to let myself think about that.

I looked at the wild little kids in my rearview mirror. "How're you doing back there?" I asked in that stupid voice even people who know better use when they're talking to kids.

Neither of them said anything. "Good to hear," I said in the same voice.

I banged a right on Beach Rose Road and headed for the yacht club. I pulled into the parking lot and drove right up next to the function room. I put the car into park, took out my keys, and kept one hand on the door. I stood on my tiptoes to look into the window. Nothing.

"Five bucks says we'll get it on the next try," I said when I got back in the car.

"Ten," one of the wild little kids said.

"Well, what do you know," I said. "You're verbal."

That got them screaming again. I rolled down my window, hoping some of the noise would escape. I thought about putting down the convertible top, since it was such a nice day, but I was afraid I might lose one of them if we hit a bump. I wanted to get rid of the wild little kids, but I also wanted to hang on to the money. They might want a partial refund for damaged children.

We backtracked, then took a left onto Inner Harbor Lane. The parking lot at the Olde Marshbury Taverne was packed. "Bingo," I said.

"I win," one of the wild little kids said behind me.

I pulled the car as close as I could to the front entrance. I left my window open a crack for air circulation and locked the car carefully. Locking kids alone in a car was probably illegal, but in my defense, abandoning them at the wrong wedding most likely was, too.

"Be right back," I said.

Almost the first person I saw was the

matron of honor. "Excuse me," I said. "But the babysitter never showed. . . ."

She looked over her shoulder. For a minute there, I thought she was going to make a run for it, but she turned back around again. "Two more hours," she said. "How much?"

Even I knew it would be bad for my self-esteem to head into Saturday night as a babysitter. "Sorry," I said.

She shook her head and followed me out to the car. The kids started screaming again when they saw her.

The matron of honor didn't thank me. I don't think she even noticed the great complimentary makeup job I'd done on her wild little offspring. She just reached into my car and unbuckled them, then started dragging them into the reception.

"You're welcome," I yelled after her.

The door to the Olde Marshbury Taverne opened, and the father of the bride emerged. He was holding Precious straight out in front of him, and he had a pile of money tucked between one hand and the dog. He walked right over to me and said something about the Board of Health. Or possibly it was the Whore of Wealth.

And then he gave me Precious, still in her cornflower blue taffeta dress with the brooch. "Sleep it," he said.

Or maybe it was, "Keep it."

Precious was standing up on my makeup kit, which I'd placed on the passenger seat of my bug, so she could see out the window. We were both pretty bored, so I offered her a drink from my water bottle. She didn't spill a drop. I had no idea dogs could be water bottle trained. After I checked carefully for moving cars, since we didn't have a leash, we went for a walk around the parking lot so she could pee again. It might have been my imagination, but she seemed grateful for the opportunity, and for a while there, I thought we were starting to bond.

Then I decided she'd probably want to do the first thing I always did after I got home from a wedding: take off the stupid, uncomfortable dress I was wearing. So I leaned over to unfasten the brooch on her dress. She growled at me.

"Whoa," I said. "Don't get testy. It was only a suggestion."

After that, we just checked each other out for a while. I had no idea what kind of dog she was, since I knew nothing about dogs. She looked kind of like a flying squirrel, except for the ears. She had the ears of a fruit bat. I wonder what she was thinking about me. Maybe she thought I had ears like a fruit bat, too.

I checked my watch. I decided that if I watched Precious for another half hour or so, I would have earned that last batch of bills. It seemed to me that there were two ways to look at things. One was that for a take-charge kind of person, I was allowing far too many things to get dumped on me. The other was that I might have no husband and no life, but I sure was making some good money today.

I reached around in the bottom of my shoulder bag and found my cell phone. I switched it from silent to ring. I looked at the screen. "Wow," I said out loud. "Two whole messages."

Precious looked over with real interest, I thought, so I held out the phone so she could hear them, too.

The first one was my mother. "Just checking in about those semiabandoned children of yours," she said. She sounded awfully perky.

I wondered what she'd say if I told her that I now had a semiabandoned dog. She'd probably just offer to get me another phone number. My mother had a number for everything.

"I'm tied up for the rest of the weekend,

honey, but Tuesday night is free if you're open."

I shook my head at Precious. "Can you believe that's my *mother?*" I whispered. "How can you be too busy for your own daughter?"

"And Bella," my mother's voice continued, "I think you should change your voice mail message. I know you're trying to be funny, but the truth is it sounds angry and bitter."

"But I *am* angry and bitter," I said to Precious. It was kind of nice having someone to talk to.

"Talk to you soon. Love you."

"Nice message," Sean Ryan's voice said suddenly. "I'll try you again later."

"Ohmigod," I said to Precious. "That was Sean Ryan."

My phone rang. I looked at it. Then I looked at Precious, and I could have sworn she nodded.

I pushed the green button. "Hello," I said.

"Hi," Sean Ryan said. "It's Sean."

"Sean," I said slowly, as if I were trying to place him. "Oh, right. The college fair guy. How'd you get my number anyway?"

"Uh, caller ID?"

There were no secrets anymore. It seemed like my best bet might be to just keep my mouth shut.

"I guess I should have checked for a message first, but I was happy to see your name, so I just pressed Call."

Precious jumped over onto my lap. She climbed her way up me until her paws were on my shoulders. She licked my cheek. I giggled.

"Am I amusing you?" Sean Ryan asked.

"No," I said. "It was someone else."

Now he wasn't saying anything.

"Listen," I said. "I just wanted to ask you a few questions about kits. Maybe I could buy you a cup of coffee one of these days? At a public restaurant?"

"Sure," he said. "As long as it's well lit."

"Okay," I said. "What town do you live in?"

"Marshbury."

"Me, too," I said. The thing about small towns is you only think you know everybody who lives there.

"Okay," he said. "How about Starbucks in ten minutes?"

"Isn't that kind of sudden?"

He laughed. "It's just that I'm not sure I could handle another phone call with you. Did anybody ever tell you you're not exactly easy to talk to?"

85

"No," I said. I looked at Precious and rolled my eyes.

8

"What is *that?*" Sean Ryan asked.

"A dog," I said. I'd put Precious in my shoulder bag so I could sneak her into Starbucks, and she was peeking out around the zipper. I was afraid the dog-in-the-purse thing might make me look like an aging Paris Hilton, which was kind of creepy, but I couldn't really think of an alternative. I probably should have brought her back into the Olde Marshbury Taverne first, but I didn't want to have to give any of the money back.

So I figured I'd just let her take the ride with me and kill some more time. It couldn't possibly take more than a half hour or so to find out about kits. Then, when we got to the Starbucks parking lot, I'd tried to leave her in my car, but she looked so sad I just couldn't do it to her.

"I meant what kind of dog," Sean Ryan said.

"No idea," I said.

Sean Ryan shook his head and smiled his crooked smile. "Moving right along," he said. He held the door to Starbucks open for me.

"Thanks," I said.

"Excuse me, Miss?" a man in a white shirt said about two seconds later. "But we don't allow dogs in here. Board of Health."

"Are you sure you don't mean Whore of Wealth?" slipped out before I thought it through.

"What?" Sean Ryan and the man in the white shirt said at exactly the same time.

"Never mind," I said. "Okay, I'll wait outside. Can you get me a grande mocha latte with skim milk and extra whipped cream?" I asked Sean Ryan. "I have money," I added.

"You'd better," he said.

We decided to walk the beach while we drank our coffee. The tide was out, and people were packing up and heading home to start dinner. Precious was having a great time, running ahead of us, then circling back to make sure we were still around. Every once in a while she'd stop and dig in the sand, or roll over on her back and wiggle around in some seaweed. Technically, she should have been on a leash, according to several prominently displayed signs, but if anyone said anything, I figured I could just stick her back in my shoulder bag.

"You're right," Sean Ryan said. "She does look a little bit like a flying squirrel. I'd guess half terrier, and maybe half Chihuahua. And probably eight pounds, soaking wet."

"Every anorexic's dream," I said. "Okay, let's talk kits."

Sean Ryan sat down and patted the sand beside him. I sat down about three feet away. He reached over and drew a line in the sand between us, and I laughed. Precious ran over to us and started digging a hole.

Suddenly, I had a mouthful of sand. While I was spitting it out, Sean Ryan picked Precious up, turned her around, and put her back down again. The sand started flying in the opposite direction.

"Thanks," I said. I put my teeth together and sand crunched between them, so I drank the rest of my latte, hoping that would help. "Okay, so how exactly did you end up test-marketing a guidance counselor's kit?" I asked.

He pushed his coffee cup into the sand so it wouldn't tip over, and leaned back on his elbows. "Well, the guidance counselor was a friend of mine back when I lived in Vermont, and he got in touch with me again when he came up with the idea."

"You used to live in Vermont?"

"Yeah, Burlington. Great place to live. Until you get divorced. Anyone you're trying to avoid, you're going to bump into every Friday night on Church Street. We didn't have any kids, so long story short, I couldn't wait to get out. You know, fresh start and all that."

Talking about former lives was so depressing. Blah. Blah. Blah. It was too bad people couldn't just shed one life and move on to the next one. No explanations, no old stories. No having to think about what went wrong and how excruciatingly painful and embarrassing it was. No need even to think at all. Just strip off one life and step into the next one.

Sean Ryan cleared his throat, and I jumped. "How long ago was that?" I asked.

He pushed himself back up and took a sip of his coffee. "About five years now."

"Did you ever throw a rock at her car?"

Sean Ryan kind of spit and snorted at the same time, and a fine spray of coffee covered us both. "Holy crap," he said. He rubbed both hands over his mouth. "Did anybody ever tell you you're dangerous?"

He reached into his pocket and pulled out a handkerchief. He handed it to me.

"I was just asking," I said. I dabbed at the parts of my face that felt wet, then gave it back to him.

He reached over and wiped a spot of coffee off my forearm. Maybe there's just something sexy about a guy who carries a handkerchief, but I had this sudden crazy urge to lean forward and kiss him. There is nothing like a good kiss on the beach.

I pulled my arm away fast. His handkerchief dangled like a white flag.

Sean Ryan shrugged and started dabbing at the dots of coffee on his own arms. "I'd have to say I'm not really a rock-throwing kind of guy," he said.

"Don't be so superior," I said.

"Okay," he said. "Antifreeze. In her coffee. But I only thought about it a couple of times."

"But you didn't actually do it?"

"I'd be in prison, wouldn't I?"

"Not if you were good at covering it up," I said.

"You really threw a rock at your ex's car?"

I nodded.

"When?"

"Ages ago," I said. "Okay, yesterday. But I

was a different person then. I've mellowed considerably."

Sean Ryan reached over to get the coffee beaded up on Precious's fur. Precious grabbed the handkerchief between her teeth and started shaking her head back and forth. Sean Ryan rolled over to his hands and knees, and they started playing tug-of-war.

Precious let go of the handkerchief and started scratching behind one ear. Sean Ryan and I both picked up our empty cups from the sand before they could blow all over the beach. "So," he said. "Is there a story to the half-sister-and-husband thing?"

"Yeah," I said. "He's now my ex-husband."

"Well, that's certainly succinct."

I didn't say anything.

He shrugged. "Okay, so what do you know about makeup that nobody else does? I mean, I'm not exactly well versed in the subject. But, say, can you just glance at people and see what would make them look better?"

"Oh, yeah. I do it constantly. It's like a switch I can't turn off. It's as if people's faces are hunks of clay, and I'd know just what I'd do with them if I were the sculptor."

Sean Ryan nodded. "That's good. Okay, say you had to put together a kit by next Saturday to teach people as much as you could about makeup. What would be in it?"

"Maybe a mirror. And some samples. And makeup brushes and disposable sponges. Ooh, and instructions for the best way to apply makeup — so many people don't have a clue how to do it, or even the right order to apply products. And a diagram of a face, so I could write down what to put where, and what brands and colors would work for them."

"Great," Sean Ryan said. "And what would the kit itself look like?"

"I don't know. Maybe kind of funky. I could use the netting you can get by the yard, you know, wrapped around and tied into a bow, maybe with a makeup brush tucked in. Or maybe it should be more of a clutch or a box or even a tote bag. I think I'll know it when I find it."

Precious started running down the beach. "I'm sure you will," Sean Ryan said. He pushed himself up to a standing position and reached his hand down to me.

I took his hand, and he pulled me up. He had a nice strong grip, but his hand was a little bit dry. Ahava made a nice hand cream just for men, but nothing worked like your basic Bag Balm. The rest of his skin was in good shape though. The eyes might be the window to your soul, but the skin was the mirror of your health. Sean Ryan's glowed like someone who took care of himself, inside and out. Maybe if I held on to his hand long enough, it would be catching.

"So now what?" I asked.

"So now you go put together a bunch of kits. I'm doing a college fair in Rhode Island a week from today. You can have half of my table."

"Thanks," I said. "Which half?"

He let go of my hand. I'd rolled up my black pants, since it was hot in the sun. I smoothed them back down. I had about five zillion pairs of black pants, and I was suddenly glad I wasn't wearing any of the ones that bagged out in the back after I'd been sitting in them.

"Which half?"

I smiled. "I just like to be on the right side. Even the chair I use at the salons has to be on the right side of the others."

"Are there any other unusual things I should know about you?"

I bent down and picked up a piece of driftwood and threw it as far as I could. Precious went flying after it, her brooch glistening in the setting sun. I kind of liked this dog thing. "Well, I never drink while I'm eating," I said.

"You mean alcohol?"

I shook my head and bent down to pick up a sand dollar. I was really in the money today. "No, anything."

Sean Ryan picked up another sand dollar and handed it right over to me. "Any particular reason? I mean, are we talking religion here? Superstition?"

"Nah, nothing like that. When we were kids, somebody was always spilling something, so we were never allowed to have drinks at the table. So now I just can't do it."

"Don't you worry about dehydration?"

"No, I just drink a lot around meals."

Sean Ryan nodded. "Ohh-kay," he said slowly.

"Come on," I said. "That's not that strange. I bet there are all sorts of odd things about you."

"Nope," he said. "I'm completely normal."

I shook my head. "Seriously doubtful."

"Let's see. I have to sleep on the right side of the bed, if that counts." He looked at me. I looked at him.

Suddenly, it was as if my sex drive hit a roadblock. Maybe I was hormonally bipolar. And, not to mix modes of transportation, but I could see where this train was heading, and I was getting off at the next stop. The mere thought of going through all that again with a whole new person left me abruptly and completely exhausted.

I caught up to Precious and scooped her into my arms.

"Was it something I said?" Sean Ryan yelled after me.

I turned around. "Listen," I yelled. "It doesn't matter what side of the bed you sleep on, because we're never going to sleep together. Got that?"

A couple walking along the beach in front of us turned around to look. Sean Ryan gave them a wave.

"For the record," he said when he caught up to me, "I wasn't asking you to sleep with me."

"Yeah, right," I said.

"I'm not even trying to sleep with you."

"You're not? Gee, thanks a lot." I knew there had to be a way to get the conversation around to something else, but I couldn't quite put my finger on it.

Sean Ryan held out his hands for Precious, and she jumped right over to him. She really did look like a flying squirrel. He held her up by his shoulder and started patting her back like he was burping a baby.

"Listen," he said. "I've already had a relationship with a recently divorced woman, and I am never going there again. So, how about you have a rebound relationship with some other guy and put him through hell. And in the meantime we can just be friends."

I put my hands on my hips. "You have absolutely no idea how long I've been divorced. And where do you get off telling me I need a rebound relationship or anything else? You've barely met me."

He stopped burping Precious and shook his head. "Hey, do you want to go get some dinner?"

"Dinner?"

"Yeah, you know, the thing you eat at night? Without drinking anything?"

"What time is it?" I asked. I was suddenly afraid to look at my watch.

"I don't know. It must be after six, though."

I grabbed Precious out of Sean Ryan's arms and got ready to run. "You don't happen to remember how long wedding receptions last, do you?"

9

"Handsome hunka burning man, that brother of yours," Esther Williams said as Mario walked by. I'd made her up before I took her pink rollers out, so a little bit of teasing and spraying and she'd be good to go for at least another week.

"Sorry, Esther," I said. "He's already married to Todd."

"They can do that now?"

"Sure they can. At least in Massachusetts. You know that."

"Damn shame. Best darn husbands you could ever have, if you put the sex on a separate platter. Good dancers, snappy dressers, some of them can even cook. It worked just fine for years. I don't know what all this new fuss is about. It's hard enough finding an eligible husband, without the gay ones cutting in on your action."

"Don't let the dog eat the dye," Vicky said behind me. I looked over my shoulder in the mirror at her.

"Good job, Vicky," I said.

Vicky was one of the developmentally challenged young adults my father hired through Road to Responsibility. We were never quite sure whether he did it to impress my mother in case she happened to hear about it, or because he somehow got a tax break. But they were great to have around. They swept the hair off the floor between customers and dusted the products on the shelves with a feather duster. They always came with a coach, who sat over in the waiting area and read magazines. If you asked me, the developmentally challenged young adults were far more productive than their coaches were.

Vicky was our favorite. She had long blond hair, alabaster skin, bow-shaped lips, and Down's syndrome. She'd had so much coaching that she now coached herself out loud all day long. The best time was when she was in the bathroom. "Just get in and get out," we'd hear her say through the closed door. "No fooling around in there. And wash your hands with soap."

"Be gentle. Don't squeeze the dog," she was saying now. Precious had a row of tiny foils running down the center of her back, and it was Vicky's job to make sure she didn't figure out a way to get to them.

Mario finally noticed the foils on Precious. "Geez, Bella, now what are you doing? You shouldn't even have a dog in here."

"Dad said it was okay for her to be here," I said, not that I'd actually asked him. "And tell Todd it didn't cost us a cent. I had extra bleach left over from my last highlight client."

"And the point would be?" Mario asked. Esther Williams put on her glasses to check out Mario, while I shook up a giant can of TIGI Bed Head Hard Head Hairspray.

"I don't know," I said. "She's got that wiry terrier undercoat, and her fur's kind of mousy. I just thought if she had a few highlights, it would tide her over until I can get her some more outfits. I finally got that bridesmaid dress off her. Let me tell you, it wasn't easy."

Precious and I had spent most of Sunday and Monday trying to track down the Silly Siren family, but they'd disappeared, lock, stock, and loose cash. The contracts they'd filled out at the Olde Taverne and the Unitarian church where they'd been married were almost completely illegible.

Mario unhooked his BlackBerry from his belt, opened the leather case, and started pushing buttons with his thumbs. "You'll probably get us shut down for animal testing," he said. "And there's a state law against even having dogs in salons, you know."

"Oh, stop," I said. "You're such a drama queen. I read somewhere there's still a Massachusetts blue law on the books prohibiting the transportation of ice, bees, and Irish moss on Sundays. I mean, how much of this stuff can you really worry about?"

"Hey," Esther Williams said. "Did anybody tell you folks about the new salon going in across the street? Under the condos, right next to those dentists? Rumor at my tango class is they're all gays."

"It's called The Best Little Hairhouse in Marshbury," Mario said.

"Seriously?" I said.

Mario nodded. "You're not planning to start cheating on us now, are you, Esther?"

Esther batted her fresh set of eyelashes. "You'd better keep a close eye on me, big boy."

"It'll be my pleasure," Mario said. He turned to me. "Just don't get attached, Bella. You know they're going to come back for it eventually."

I looked over at Precious. She was sitting quietly and offering a paw to Vicky. I couldn't wait to finish up Esther so I could get those foils out before they damaged any fur. Good thing she was small enough to shampoo in one of the sinks, though I probably should do it in the utility sink in the back, instead of in one of the sinks we used for customers. At least if Mario was still here. And I'd use a good conditioner, maybe Redken All Soft Conditioner for Dry and Brittle Hair. And, after that, a touch of John Frieda SOS Magic Anti-Frizz Gloss Serum, just over the highlights, where she couldn't lick it off.

"Oh, please," I said. "I'm so not attached. I only bought a week's worth of food for her. And she's not an *it,* by the way. She's a *she.*"

Mario looked up from his BlackBerry. "Just make sure you don't bring her with you tonight."

I started spraying Esther's hair, and she started waving her hand back and forth in front of her face. "What's tonight?" I asked.

"The senate candidates are debating live on *Beantown* at seven? Try reading your schedule once in a while, why don't you."

"*Beantown* isn't my job. It's . . ." I didn't even want to say her name, so I just didn't.

"Sophia can't do both of them, Bella. Their people don't want them in the same room before the debate. So they're setting up a second green room."

"No way. Send somebody else."

"Bella, come on. I need you. You've already made up the governor, and we didn't get a complaint."

I realized I was still spraying Esther Williams, who was good to go for at least a month now, even in a hurricane. I put the hairspray down. I ran my hands through my own hair while I tried to think of a good way out. I couldn't. "Okay, I'll do it. As long as I don't have to be in the same room as you know who. And I want the good candidate this time."

"Bella, come on. Sophia's been doing him for years."

"I'm not even going to touch that line, Mario."

Mario grinned. "Okay. Let me see what I can do."

I unfastened the Velcro on Esther Williams's cape and lifted it off her. Mario put his hand under her elbow as she stood, and she tilted her head up so she could gaze into his eyes. Precious came bouncing over to me. I swooped down and picked her up.

"All right, I'll do it," I said. "As long as you and Todd are available to babysit."

"Bella, it's a *dog.* You can leave it alone for a few hours."

I started to take out Precious's foils. "Nonnegotiable," I said.

I was pissed. Leave it to Sophia to get in there first and spread out her stuff all over the place and completely take over the real makeup room. It was only about the size of a medium walk-in closet, but it was connected to the green room at the public television station that produced *Beantown.* It had a long rectangular vanity that took up the entire length of one wall. The vanity had a strip of fairly decent lighting up near the ceiling, and there was even a hydraulic chair, plus an extra regular chair in the corner to put stuff on. The doorway was positioned in such a way that you could watch TV at the same time you were doing makeup, and there was even a coffeemaker.

I, on the other hand, had been shuttled down the hall to a makeshift green room. And not only that, but it was in the men's bathroom, or at least almost in the men's bathroom. It was actually a small room that was a walk-through to the men's bathroom. It was about half the size of the real makeup room, with a row of small school-like lockers on one wall and a short counter with a dirty mirror over it on the opposite wall. Lousy lighting. No television. No coffeemaker. Mario would be hearing about this, that was for sure.

I went stomping back down the hall to get a chair, because of course it didn't even have one of those. If Sophia hadn't been sitting in the hydraulic chair, staking her claim, I would have just commandeered that and dragged it down the hallway, but I couldn't be bothered dumping her out of it first. I grabbed the chair in the corner.

"Do you need help?" she asked.

"Not from you," I said.

I carried the chair back to my makeshift dungeon. I waited. I waited some more. Finally, the senator-running-for-reelection came walking down the hallway with his people. My dungeon door was open, of course, because I probably would have suffocated to death in there if I tried closing it.

I stuck my head through the doorway and gave them my most dazzling smile. "Hi," I said. "I'm all set for you in here."

The senator-running-for-reelection just kept walking. His people kept walking, too. One of them, possibly the bodyguard, looked over at me briefly. It was hard to tell if he was checking me out because I looked good or because I was a potential security threat.

I leaned sideways against the doorframe

and watched them head for the real green room, the real makeup room, and Sophia. She always got everything. It was completely unfair. And the most awful part about it was that I was probably the one responsible for it. I was pretty sure I had turned Sophia into the person she'd become.

I was twelve, right in the midst of that quick little window of time that's the golden age for babysitters, when Sophia was born. A few years earlier and I would still have been too much of a kid myself. A couple years later and I would have moved on to chasing boys.

I was obsessed with her. I changed her, bathed her, fed her, dressed her up like a doll, pushed her all over the neighborhood in her stroller. I ignored her mother, my father's new wife. I might have even seen myself as Sophia's real mother, or at least her minimom.

Sophia's eyes lit up every time I walked in the door to my father's house from school. Divorce wasn't yet the norm back then, and my mother had taken the even more unusual step of moving out of the family home. She bought a small house in a neighboring town, closer to college for her, but in a lesser school district.

Mario, Angela, and I spent most nights at

her house. Angela and I were jammed into one tiny bedroom in bunk beds, and Mario had an even tinier room all to himself. Dinner, homework, bed, then breakfast. Then she drove us to school in Marshbury. After school, we took the school bus home to our old rooms and old father, his latest new wife, and eventually, Sophia. I gladly gave up half my room, and at least half my life, to her.

Mario was eleven months older than I was, and Angela thirteen months younger. Either Mario and I or Angela and I would have been considered Irish twins. Put us all together, and I guess we were pseudo Italian Irish triplets. Mario spent most of his time ignoring me, and I spent most of my time ignoring Angela, who spent most of her time ignoring our younger half sister, Tulia.

So Sophia, the youngest, got all my attention. I put ribbons in her hair, nail polish on her toes, taught her to sing "Twinkle, Twinkle, Little Star" and to play "Trot Trot to Boston." And when I outgrew the babysitting years, my friends and I still let her go everywhere with us. Shopping, football games, at least the first few hours of every sleepover.

Somewhere along the line, I think I ruined

her. She looked like me, she dressed like me, she acted like me. I went to UMass to major in art, and then twelve years later, so did she. I circled back to work for my father after a brief stop at Blaine Beauty School. Eventually, so did she.

I don't think she ever learned to think for herself. I should have insisted, instead of letting her follow me through life like a little human chameleon who changed her colors to match mine. I couldn't even enjoy hating her guts without feeling guilty, because I had to be at least partly responsible for the fact that she needed to have everything that I had, including my husband. And if all that wasn't bad enough, I really missed her.

10

A few minutes before seven, after the producer had trotted back to my dungeon at least three times looking for him, a little more frantically each time, the governor-running-for-senator and his people finally showed. I jumped up from the uncomfortable little chair and grabbed my airbrush gun. The governor's people stayed in the hallway. The governor walked right by me without saying anything. A moment later I heard him peeing in the next room.

"Oh, boy," I said out loud. I took what might well have been the fastest three steps I've ever taken in my life out to the hallway.

"Where did you come from?" a woman asked. It was the same woman who'd been with him at the governor's mansion, so I guessed she wasn't the housekeeper after all. Maybe she was the governorkeeper. She reached past me to shut the door. She was wearing a black skirt tonight, and I was happy that I'd at least been right about that. The black made her look like she had perfectly balanced buttocks, with barely a hint of visible panty line anywhere.

"Um," I said. "Actually, they've made that a makeup room. My stuff is already in there."

The man next to her pushed the door back open. "Well, I'd sure like to know where the other candidate is being made up," he said. "And don't think I won't find out."

The producer came jogging down the hallway. "Ten minutes," she yelled.

"Don't worry," I said. "He only needs four."

We all walked back in when we heard the toilet flush. Perhaps the governor got nervous before televised debates. Maybe his dinner hadn't agreed with him. In any case, I held my breath as best I could as I airbrushed him.

"Jesus," one of his people said. "I'll meet you out in the hallway."

"Mirror," the governor said four minutes later, after I'd dusted him quickly with some extra powder. Nothing looks worse on HDTV than shine.

"He wants a mirror," the governorkeeper said.

I angled the mirror up at him. He nodded, then finally looked at me. "I'd appreciate your vote in November," he said as he reached his hand out to me.

I picked up my airbrush gun again fast and just nodded. I hadn't heard the sink turn on in there. Governor or no governor, there was no way I was shaking that hand.

There were two chairs waiting for the candidates on the *Beantown* set. The *Beantown* host and two reporters holding notepads sat directly across from them. They were already in full television makeup. I wondered if Sophia had done it. It didn't take a genius to figure out she'd probably hogged them all.

After a brief fight by the candidates' people about which candidate got which chair, there was barely time to attach the microphones and do a quick sound check.

Sophia leaped forward and gave her candidate a quick, and totally unnecessary, I thought, pat on his forehead with a makeup sponge. I ran up there, too, just so I wouldn't look like a slacker, and flicked a bit of lint off my candidate's suit jacket.

"Clear the set," some guy said to me in a really mean voice.

"Sor-ry," I said.

"We're live in three, two, one," he said,

and then the goofy *Beantown* theme music came on, and the *Beantown* host started smiling her big, toothy smile. I was standing right next to Sophia, which wasn't exactly the most comfortable place I could imagine being. I also couldn't think of a less interesting thing to do than listen to two politicians debate.

When I was married to Craig, he used to rant and rave a lot about politics. I might have even faked political passion a few times, the way some women fake orgasm. But the truth was, I'd never really bought into the whole thing.

The way it looked to me was that they were all basically liars, so what was even the point? Why not simply outlaw having political parties and just make everybody work together, sort of like when I was back in elementary school and dodgeball was briefly replaced by team-building New Games. Instead of fighting for office, the candidates could simply join hands and say, "We *both* win." Then they could donate the money they would have spent on ads and fancy dinners and use it to go stop global warming or fill some potholes or something. Cooperation, not competition, was what we needed in the world today.

At the commercial break, I broke into a

sprint so I could get to my candidate before Sophia got to hers. I fluffed him up fast, then headed over with my Angel blush to one of the reporters. If Sophia thought she was getting all of them, she had another thing coming.

The reporter covered up his notebook as I approached him. Like I'd bother to copy his work. "That's not blush, is it?" he asked.

"Don't worry," I lied. "It's only bronzer."

"I'll take some of that," the guy next to him said. "I had a great tan at the beginning of the summer, but it sure doesn't take long to fade, does it?"

"Clear the set," the same mean guy said. "We're live in three, two, one. . . ."

I found a place a bit farther away from Sophia this time. I crossed my arms and leaned back against a wall. I also didn't quite get the whole U.S. senator thing. I mean, why should Massachusetts pay to send somebody all the way to Washington, instead of keeping him here, where it seemed to me there was more than enough work to be done? Fixing the tunnels and bridges alone could take a term or two.

These guys were particularly boring, even for politicians. If you smooshed them both together into one person, they still wouldn't have enough combined charisma to get elected to anything, if you asked me. As soon as I glanced up at the monitors I could see that neither of them was all that photogenic on television either. Makeup could help, but life was tough — the camera either loved you or it didn't. Some cultures thought a camera could steal your soul. I knew for sure it could steal your beauty.

They kept droning on and on until eventually *Beantown* was over. I headed back to the men's bathroom to pack up my kit. I couldn't wait to get to Mario and Todd's to see how Precious was doing. They were responsible enough, but she was probably really missing me by now.

"Bella," I heard Sophia say behind me just as I was entering my dungeon.

I turned. "What?" I said.

Sophia took a few more steps toward me. She looked like she was wading through knee-high water. Then she just stood there, giving me her sad sack look, as if she were still in fourth grade and the kids had been mean to her at school that day. She had dark circles under her eyes, though for all I knew, maybe even they weren't real.

What I did know, beyond a shadow of a doubt, was that she was waiting for me to make the first move, to invite her out for a drink, to make it easy for her to finally apologize. To help her talk things through, to find a way to do the impossible and work things out between us.

She raised her shoulders and then dropped them again. She opened her mouth. She closed her mouth. She licked her lips.

I just couldn't do it for her this time. I turned my back on her and went into my dungeon. I fumbled in my makeup case until I found the lipstick I needed: Sheer Ice.

My mother opened the door to Mario and Todd's house when I rang the bell.

"Hi, Mom," I said. I leaned forward and kissed her, then reached back to shut the door. "I thought you weren't free till Tuesday. I was going to call you."

"It is Tuesday," my mother said. I loved her, but she had this annoying habit of always being right.

My mother looked great, as usual. Her hair was coarse and gray and wavy, and while she never left the house without red lipstick, it was the only makeup she ever wore.

I tilted my head to get a better look at her red satin lips. "That's a new color," I said. "I like it. What is it?"

My mother smiled. "Lover," she said, "by

Chanel."

Precious came running out to greet me, and my heart did a little thump. "Oh, baby," I said as I picked her up for a hug. "I missed you so much."

"I see what you mean," my mother said to Mario and Todd.

"What?" I said.

"Bella," Mario said. "It's just that there's no sense getting attached to a dog that isn't yours."

"Look who's talking," I said. I held Precious away from me so I could read her new T-shirt. It was pink, in a nice combed cotton, and it said HOOCHIE POOCHIE in rhinestones. "At least she's closer to being mine than she is yours."

"You're welcome," Mario said. He opened the oven and pulled out a foil-wrapped plate of whatever they'd just had for dinner and put it on a place mat on the dining island for me. A wineglass with a partially eaten scoop of sorbet sat in the center of each of the other three place mats. I put Precious on the floor, and Todd handed me a knife and fork and a cloth napkin.

Mario and Todd were a good team. Todd balanced the books for our family business, and Mario came up with the ideas. Mario cooked, Todd cleaned up. Todd was the

116

carpenter, Mario the decorator. Todd helped Andrew with his math, and Mario taught him how to dress. They were both great parents.

"Do you think I would have had better luck as a lesbian?" I asked.

Mario and my mother gave each other a look. "You take it," my mother said.

Mario nodded. "No," he said, "I think you would have had better luck if you'd chosen a partner who wasn't a self-absorbed jerk."

Todd reached into a bag on the kitchen counter and held up another tiny T-shirt, this one turquoise. "YOU HAD ME AT WOOF," he read out loud. "We tried to get this one for you, too, but they were out of human sizes."

"That's okay," I said. I took a bite of some kind of spicy shrimp and rice thing. "Mmm, this is good."

Todd reached back in and pulled out KARMA'S A BITCH in black and white, along with DON'T HATE ME BECAUSE I'M BEAUTIFUL in a soft yellow with cougar print accents.

"You guys are unbelievable," I said. "Wait till you're grandfathers — Andrew's kids are going to be spoiled rotten."

Mario and Todd looked at each other.

"Grandfathers," they both moaned.

"Oh, stop whining," my mother said. "It's far less painful than you'd think." She took another bite of her sorbet.

"I'm looking forward to the baby part," Mario said. "It's just the title that's going to take some getting used to. Like adding several decades to your image."

"Let's finish worrying about the wedding first," Todd said. "Then we let Amy get pregnant. Then we can move on to your image."

"Well, the wedding will be here before you know it," my mother said. "It doesn't seem possible it's a week from Saturday."

As much as I was dying to see my nephew get married, I was worried about one thing. I tried to make my voice sound casual. "She wouldn't dare bring him, would she?"

Todd and Mario looked at each other. "Just ignore them," Mario said. "It'll be fine."

I couldn't believe it. "How could you?" I said. "How could you let her bring Craig to Andrew's wedding? I mean, what if you and Todd broke up and he wanted to bring a date?"

"He's Andrew's dad," Mario said. "He'd have that right."

Todd just shrugged, so I turned to my mother.

My mother laughed. "Don't go there with me. I've had to take the high road with your father a time or two. Just move on, honey. Bring your own date, if it will make you feel better." She took a bite of sorbet, then looked up. "Who knows, I might just decide to bring one of my own."

Mario and I looked at each other. I wondered whose eyes were wider.

11

"A date?" Mario said. "At Andrew's wedding?"

"You can't do that," I said. "Dad would die."

My mother laughed. "Don't worry. Your father would be thrilled for me."

"Yeah, right," I said. Even though we all knew my father was responsible for the breakup of all three of his marriages, for some reason he was the one we worried about when it came to my mother. Maybe because she was so strong, and he'd always seemed more hurt than she was when it ended. I should probably feel differently, now that I knew what it felt like to be cheated on, but he was my dad, and I loved him.

"You know, Mom," Mario said. "He still wants to be buried with you."

"Over my dead body," my mother said. This cracked us all up, so we just laughed for a while. My mother could be a pain, but I also had to admit she could be pretty funny sometimes, too.

"Actually, I think that's his exact fantasy," I said. "He wants you to die together like Romeo and Juliet. He brings it up every time he goes for that third glass of Chianti."

Mario nodded. "Yeah, and then he gets up and does his death scene. It's not quite Shakespeare, but it sure is dramatic."

My mother smiled. She looked relaxed and radiant. Whoever this guy was would be lucky to have her. My mother hadn't dated much over the years, at least as far as we knew. There was a guy from Boston way back, and then a principal from a local high school a few years ago. She seemed genuinely happy on her own. I wondered if I'd ever get there.

I took a final bite of dinner and got up and put my plate in the sink. Now that I could drink something, I opened the refrigerator and poured myself a glass of one percent milk. I held up the carton for any takers. Everybody shook their heads, so I put it back in the refrigerator.

"Do you think there's a statute of limitations on infidelity?" I asked after I sat back down again. "I mean, just in general?"

My mother stirred her sorbet around in

her wineglass. We all watched her. Precious picked up a chew toy and brought it over to me so I could throw it across the room for her. So far, it seemed to be her favorite game.

"In western Europe," my mother finally said, "and the United States, only about four out of ten people think infidelity is unforgivable. In Turkey, it's nine out of ten. So it's all perspective. You have to figure it out for yourself, Bella."

I threw the chew toy a little bit harder than I meant to, and it almost took out a lamp. Todd cringed but didn't say anything.

"We're not talking about me," I said.

"Of course we are," my mother said.

"Fine," I said. "I'm totally Turkish. What about you?"

My mother shrugged. "Some betrayals are so big, how could you ever trust the person again? So you sit with it for a while, then you find a way to move on."

"I'm working up to it," I said. "I really am."

"Hey, speaking of Dad," Mario said, "Todd thinks we should try to get him to cut his hair for the wedding."

"Thanks, throw me under the bus," Todd said. "And I'm not so sure it's even a good idea. If everybody is busy watching the pseudo Italian Donald Trump, you and I might not attract as much attention."

I took a sip of my milk. "Are you worried about that?" I asked.

Todd smiled. "At a big Southern wedding? In a conservative state like Georgia? Nah."

"Actually, Atlanta's pretty much the gay capital of the South," Mario said. "And Amy's parents seemed only moderately freaked-out when we flew down to meet them. Bottom line, if Andrew and Amy are fine, then we're fine."

"I know," my mother said. "You can stage an intervention."

"Huh?" we all said at once.

My mother smiled. "We help families do it all the time at work. You know, everybody writes a letter saying how the behavior, or in this case, the hair, has negatively impacted their lives, and then they corner the person and confront him respectfully but forcefully with tough-love ultimatums."

I felt a little glimmer of excitement. It was nice to know I could still feel enthusiasm about something. "Sounds like fun," I said. "I'm so in."

Mario and Todd looked at each other. "Us, too," Mario said. "How about Friday night at the meeting?"

"Mom?" I asked.

"Not a chance," she said. "Lucky Shaughnessy's hair is not my problem anymore."

My mother and I walked out together, and Precious stopped to pee in Mario and Todd's manicured side yard.

"Are you sure she should be doing that here?" my mother asked.

"It's good fertilizer," I said. "Wow, will you look at all those stars."

"Remember when you were little and I was showing you how to find the Big Dipper, and you asked me what kind of dip it was?" my mother asked.

I nodded. "I was hoping for spinach, I think." Precious trotted over and stretched out at my feet. I bent down to scratch the top of her head. "Mom, did you ever look back and wonder if things could have been different between you and Dad?"

My mother kept looking up at the stars. "Sure. Once you get past the first bloom, marriage takes a lot of work. You know that. And we had three small children, when we were still essentially children ourselves. Your father wanted his dreams to be my dreams. I wanted my own dreams, so I went back to school to finish my degree, one class at a time. He wanted me to major in business to help the salon. I wanted to be a social worker to get away from the salon. So, business at the salon picked up and your father hired more stylists, attractive stylists, willing to share both his dreams and his bed. And the rest is ancient history."

I stood up and crossed my arms over my chest. It was a long time ago, but I still remembered my parents' yelling like it was yesterday. "Do you ever wish you could rewind everything and try again?"

"Not anymore," my mother said. "Life was so exhausting back then. It's much simpler now." She leaned over and gave me a kiss on my forehead. "I know it's hard to move past all the hurt, the embarrassment. But don't give up on love, honey. Next time around you'll know who you are and what you want your life to be. My best advice is to give yourself some time to heal, then jump back in with both feet."

Precious and I stopped by Salon de Paolo on the way home. This was easy, since I lived in the apartment over it. In some roundabout way involving a trust my father had set up, I would eventually own both the salon and the apartment. Right now I paid a reduced rent on the apartment in return for keeping an eye out for potential shampoo robbers below.

This arrangement had always really bothered Craig when we were married. Craig's wife had bought out his half of their house when they divorced, and Craig had bought a small condo in Boston. He started renting it out when we got married.

We'd had many discussions over the years about whether my father should sign the building over to me, so Craig, as my husband, could get his name on it, too. Not that Craig had ever gotten around to putting my name on his condo.

Craig thought my father was controlling. My father thought Craig was a salon hunter. I supposed it was true poetic justice that Sophia lived over another of my father's salons and Craig wouldn't be able to get his name on that one either. In a couple of centuries, I might even think it was funny that he'd ended up with her.

I unlocked the door to Salon de Paolo and switched Precious to my other arm so I could reach the lights. After work today I'd gone through the junk drawers in the back room of Salon de Lucio, where we kept our airbrush equipment and most of our makeup. I found a few things for my kits, including a big box of clear plastic pop-top containers. As soon as I figured out what to put in them, I could paint *B*s for *Bella* on the top of each one with chocolate brown nail polish.

I was rifling through one of the shelves in the back room when I hit the jackpot: four sixteen-ounce bottles of wholesale generic foundation ranging from porcelain to chestnut. They'd never been opened. They'd probably been sitting here for years, since they were sandwiched between a box of old metal bobby pins and a basket of hair crimpers we probably hadn't touched since 1993. Maybe Mario had picked them up at a makeup show to use as backup, and then he'd forgotten all about them.

The foundation had separated a bit, though as soon as I shook it up, it was as good as new. I opened one of the bottles to check for an off smell, but it was fine. Apparently foundation didn't spoil the way lipstick did. Most people don't know that they should always sniff their lipsticks before they buy them. Even though it still looks the same, lipstick gets a funny taste and smell once it's past its prime. When we were kids, we all used to fight about who got to keep the old lipstick, since we couldn't sell it after a couple of years. You just learned to breathe through your mouth and not to lick your lips when you were wearing it.

I'd found enough foundation to make

maybe a hundred kits, which would save me a ton of money. I could mix the shades together, and give each person a little pop-top container of her own custom-blended foundation as part of their kit. Celebrities paid big bucks for this kind of thing. Even at a college fair, I should be able to get at least $29.95.

I called Precious, and she came to me right away. It was amazing how quickly she'd become a good dog once we'd started hanging out together. She hadn't nipped at anybody or peed on the floor once. I wondered if it worked both ways. Maybe eventually I'd become a better person, too. One could always hope.

I turned out the lights and locked the front door. Precious followed me around to the side of the building. I unlocked the door to my separate entrance, and we headed up the stairs to my apartment. My sister, Angela, had helped me pick out a rich beachy color called Coral Essence for the front door. The stairway walls were just a shade or two lighter.

For some reason, even though I'd studied art in college, I was much better at picking out colors for people than I was for walls. But the right door color could make you glad you were home, and Coral Essence did that for me. Angela and I had never had much in common. She was usually busy driving her two kids to their soccer games, so we didn't spend much time together. She worked a few days a week for my father, but her real life was all about P.T.O. meetings and dinner parties, and neither was exactly my cup of tea. But I could always count on her in a decorating crisis. And she'd never once put the moves on my husband.

It was so quiet when I pushed the door open to my apartment. I hadn't gotten used to that yet. I wished we had a techno geek in the family, someone who could wire the front door so that an excited voice exclaimed, "Bella! Welcome home!" every time I entered my apartment. Maybe the fireplace could light, too. And a garden fountain, something in a tasteful copper with a nice verdigris finish, could turn on out on the balcony.

I put Precious's big shopping bag on the floor in the kitchen and filled up her ceramic water bowl. While she lapped happily, I carried her new wardrobe down the hallway to my bedroom. I couldn't manage to hang her tiny T-shirts on my hangers, since the armholes were too close together, but I folded them over the bottom rungs of the hangers and spaced them evenly across

Craig's side of the closet. I took a step back and tried to decide whether Precious's clothes made Craig's side of the closet look more or less sad and empty.

I washed my face. I brushed my teeth. I moisturized. I flopped down on the right side of my bed.

Sleep is our best friend. While we sleep, our bodies go into repair mode. Sleep regenerates our skin, which is why dark circles under our eyes are the first sign of sleep deprivation.

As I stared up at the ceiling, I knew better than to count sheep, because contrary to popular belief, all that math actually stimulates the brain. The calcium and tryptophan in the milk I'd had earlier should be helping me relax, but I wasn't feeling it.

I closed my eyes. I felt around on my bedside table until I located my Burt's Bees Replenishing Lip Balm with Pomegranate Oil. I massaged it slowly into my lips without opening my eyes.

Precious came running into the room, her toenails clicking on the oak floors. I wondered if she needed them trimmed. She might even enjoy some polish. She jumped up on the bed and snuggled in beside me.

When my cell phone rang, I felt like I was underwater and didn't have the energy to kick my way to the surface. I let it ring until it stopped. My house phone rang next, on the table, right beside my ear. I couldn't see the caller ID from this position. I thought about twisting around so I could see it, but it felt like way too much effort. It rang again. And again. Precious jumped on my stomach and gave me a worried look.

"Okay, okay," I said. I reached over and picked up the phone. "Bella's Beauty Bag," I said, just to try out the sound of it for my kits.

"Bella," the voice on the phone sobbed. "It's Lizzie," she added, as if I wouldn't know Craig's daughter's voice anywhere.

I sat up fast, and Precious went sliding off me like I was a ski slope. I reached out to pet her, so she'd know it was an accident. "Lizzie, honey," I said. "What's wrong?" For a second I had this crazy idea that Craig was dead, though everything in me knew I couldn't get that lucky.

She kept sobbing. I'd known her long enough to just wait it out. "I'm right here, Lizzie," I whispered.

Finally, she took a deep, ragged breath. "My mother sucks," she said.

"Where are you?" I asked.

"At school."

"Already? That's early."

"Whatever. She thinks I should be on the premed track, but whose life is it anyway. And I totally know what I want now. They have the best culinary arts major here. I could have my own show on the Food Network. I even have a name for it — *Radiator Ramen Noodles and Other Rad Recipes for College Survival.*" She sniffed loudly in my ear.

"Wow," I said carefully. "That's a really interesting idea."

"I knew you'd get it," she said. "Can you talk to my dad about it? He's being such a loser."

Craig had moved out over a year ago. I knew teenagers were self-absorbed, but she had to have noticed we weren't together anymore. "Lizzie," I said. "I don't think I'm the best person to talk to your dad. Maybe . . ." I reached hard for a maybe.

"Don't even say it," Lizzie said. "Sophia's a total bitch." She sniffed again and let out a little sob, possibly a bit forced this time. "Please?" she added in the little girl voice I'd never been able to resist.

12

Tulia brought her kids to the meeting early, and settled them in chairs, since all three of them needed haircuts. Today both Tulia and the kids were dressed in jeans and white T-shirts, so possibly she'd gone from color coding her children to creating a full family uniform. I made a mental note to ask Mario for his opinion on this later.

A few of the stylists had come in before the meeting started to practice some new twists on French braids. One of them, who had tiny seashells hot glued to hairpins and worked into her braid, was poking chopsticks through a braid she'd just finished on the stylist in front of her. I listened to them buzzing about The Best Little Hairhouse in Marshbury while they worked. I wondered if any of them would head across the street to find out if the grass was greener. Hairstylists are almost as nomadic as gypsies.

Sophia and her mother, Linda, aka ex-wife

C, showed up early, too, and Sophia was doing a full foil on her mother's hair. A timer went off, and Sophia opened a foil to check the progress, then began taking out the rest of them.

"Are those lowlifes?" one of the stylists asked.

I looked at Sophia. "You betcha," I said before I thought it through.

Sophia gave me a dirty look. "Takes one to know one," she said.

"Ooh," I said. "That's mature."

"Low *lights,*" Sophia's mother, Linda, said, pronouncing it carefully, as if she were teaching the stylist a new language. Mario, Angela, and I used to imitate just this sort of thing when we were younger. "Low *lights*" I could imagine us mouthing behind her back. We'd never understood what my father had seen in her. Tulia's flaky mother, Didi, had been a lot easier to take when she came along a few years earlier. She didn't try to teach us a thing. She ignored us and hung out with our father, which was just fine with us.

My father had been single again for years. Life went on, and both Tulia's and Sophia's moms were remarried and back working for us. I didn't think much of it until I'd gone off to college and was sitting around with some new friends, describing our families. *Wow,* they all said, *and I thought my family was screwed up.*

"Every family has something," my social worker mother said when I mentioned it to her at fall break. "And, believe you me, most of my clients would trade places with you in a heartbeat."

It's hard to mess up a haircut on thick, wavy hair, but Tulia was managing it. Her daughter Maggie's hair was now shoulder length on one side only. Tulia had the dark hair and pale skin of the rest of the Shaughnessy clan, but she sure hadn't inherited the hand-eye coordination. As soon as she finished trimming Maggie's hair, Angela took her niece by the hand to another chair to even it out.

Tulia moved on to her oldest child, Mack. After just a few snips, one of his ears was half covered with hair, and the other one was completely visible. His bangs tilted downhill from left to right.

Mario walked over and casually took the scissors out of Tulia's hands.

"What?" Tulia said.

Mario just shook his head and started doing damage control. Mack looked so much like Mario had at that age. Whenever I saw them together, I felt like I was watching one of those split-screen computer projections showing what a child will look like when he grows up. I hoped Mack turned out to be as good a big brother to Maggie as Mario was to me.

My father made his grand entrance through the breezeway door. His black, black hair was moussed and stretched evenly over his scalp. His Cover Your Bald Spot Instantly was living up to its promise. My father, who prided himself on having a new look at each meeting, was wearing black leather pants, a black T-shirt, and a salmon cotton sweater tied around his shoulders.

"Are you sure he's not gay?" Todd whispered to Mario.

"Focus," I whispered. We'd all worked hard on our notes, and we were ready for our hair intervention. The plan was to let him start the meeting and then jump in when he asked if we had anything else to bring up.

My father walked right over to Sophia's mother, Linda. He reached for her hand and bowed from the waist to kiss it. *"Carissima,"* he said, still holding her hand. "You get more beautiful every time I see you."

She smiled up at him. "Oh, you," she said.

My father smiled back. He was a great guy

to date, even a great guy to be divorced from. He just didn't do so well in the space between the two. He let go of her hand and started snapping his fingers, and we all started dragging our chairs into a semicircle.

Sophia walked in front of me. I figured the sound of the dragging chairs, not to mention the commotion my father always brought along with him, would mask our conversation. "Hey," I said. "When you see Craig, tell him to call me, okay?"

There was a sudden dead silence in the room.

"About *what?*" Sophia asked.

"Not that it's any of your business, but it's about Lizzie."

I was pretty sure I saw a flash of jealousy, and I took a moment to savor it. "What about Lizzie?" she asked.

I shrugged. "Just tell him to call. Or not."

I turned my back on her just in time to see Precious running over to my father. She screeched to a halt in front of him, sat, and offered her paw. My father ignored her. Precious stood up again and jumped. Repeatedly. She was an amazingly good jumper and managed to get her tiny self up almost to eye level with my six-foot-tall father.

"Is that a dog in my salon?" my father asked.

"Nope," I said.

"Good thing," my father said, with just a hint of the half-smirk we all called his Mona Lisa smile. Precious put everything she had into her next leap, and this time he caught her just before she started heading back down. He held her away from him so he could read her KARMA'S A BITCH T-shirt. "No shit," he said.

Precious tilted her head and looked at him. My father handed Precious over to me. "It's about time you got some new companionship," he said. "Much better looking than that hound dog you were married to, by the way."

"Now, now, Lucky," Sophia's mother, Linda, said.

My father opened the breezeway door and picked up something covered with a sheet. He walked back to us. He waited to make sure we were all looking. Then he waited a little longer to heighten the drama. Finally, he whipped the sheet off with a flourish. The hand-carved sign he held up read THE BEST LITTLE HAIRHOUSE IN MARSH-BURY.

Everybody gasped. "Da-ad," Angela said. "Put that back. Right now."

My father grinned. "Hey, what else could

I do? It's false advertising. Everybody knows we're the best little hairhouse in this town."

"Well, we've certainly got one hair working here, that's for sure," I mumbled, not quite under my breath.

"Speak for yourself," Sophia said.

It got a little bit quiet after that. Mario jumped in to cover the silence and get us back on track. "Dad," he said. "You can't do that."

"I just did, sonny boy. Good thing they didn't have it nailed down yet." My father touched his head lightly with one hand to make sure his hair was still in place. "Don't worry, they'll never miss it. I put a NO PARKING sign in its place."

Todd was on his feet now. "Give me the sign, Lucky," he said. "We don't need a lawsuit here."

"They're the ones who'd better look out for a lawsuit," my father said. "If they think they can bamboozle me into selling this salon, they've got another thing coming. I know who's giving my name to all those real estate barracudas."

"How much are they offering?" I asked.

"That's enough out of you, Angela," my father said.

"Bella," I said.

"There's not enough money in the world,"

my father said.

Todd held out his hand. "Give me the sign, Lucky."

My father shrugged and handed him the sign, and Todd headed out the salon door with it.

"Okay, now settle down, everybody," my father said, even though he was the only one causing trouble, in my opinion. "We've got some serious competition moving in across the street. You're all going to have to start dressing a little spiffier around here. Especially the boys, if you catch my drift." He did a few exaggerated steps in his leather pants, then executed a pretty convincing runway turn.

That did it. Mario was on his feet. "Dad," he said. "The meeting's over. This is an intervention."

Angela and I got my father into a chair and half hugged, half leaned on him to keep him there. Tulia went over to get her kids from the kiddie area.

"Mamma mia!" my father yelled.

"Holy cannoli!" he added when Todd came back in and locked the salon door.

"What the hell is going on here?" he finally said, having pretty much exhausted his Italian vocabulary.

"Dad," Angela said. "We just want you to

listen to us, okay?"

"You're all fired," my father said. Tulia's kids looked up with wide eyes. All three of them were holding pieces of paper in their hands. "And the three young whipper-snappers over there are grounded," my father said in their direction.

We had a script, so we all knew the little kids were going first to soften him up. "Nonno's only kidding," Tulia said. My father, of course, insisted that his grandchildren call him by the Italian word for grandpa. "Go ahead now."

Mack, Maggie, and Myles stepped forward. Only Mack could read so far, but the other two opened their papers, as if they could. "Nonno," Mack said. "We love you very much. We think your hair looks very funny. Please cut it."

Maggie held up an unidentifiable crayon drawing. "Nonno," she said. "This is you being handsome without fake hair."

Myles started giggling and toddled back to his mother with his paper.

Vicky, our favorite developmentally challenged young adult from Road to Responsibility, had stayed for the intervention, too. Her coach looked up from her magazine, but Vicky didn't need her. "Just say it out loud," Vicky said. "And speak up." She opened up a crumpled piece of paper. "Haircuts don't hurt one bit," she said. "You don't even need a Band-Aid." Then she giggled and sat down.

Angela tightened her grip when I let go of my father. I reached into my pocket for my note. It had all seemed like a big joke to me, but now I was surprised to feel so much emotion. "In the second grade," I began, "we started hiding your Cover Your Bald Spot Instantly spray. By junior high we'd moved on to trying to replace your shampoo with Nair. This didn't mean we didn't love you, or that we didn't think you were handsome. It's just that your hair is the first thing you see when you come into a room, and we think it's time to let it go. Plus, think of all the time it'll free up."

"Easy for you to say," my father said. "It's no hair off your head. And that Samson fellow should be a lesson for all of us. He was from Italy, you know."

"No he wasn't," I said. "He was from Israel."

My father never tired of trying to make the whole world Italian. "Well, then the guy who painted him was."

A picture from my long-ago art history class appeared before my very eyes. "Wait," I said. "You're right. There was that great

142

brown ink Guercino did. The one where Samson points to his bald spot."

"I don't have a bald spot once I cover it," my father said. "That's the whole point."

"Can we try to stay on track here?" Todd said.

Mario already had his note out. "You know, Dad," he began, "when Mom suggested this intervention —"

"Sweet Italy," my father said. "Why didn't you tell me it was her idea?"

13

Once my father made the decision, there was no stopping him. He decided to go for the full Kojak look. "Lollipops," he said, while I removed his salmon sweater from his shoulders, and Todd draped a black cape over him. "Somebody go find me some lollipops."

I wasn't sure what Sinéad O'Connor's method had been, but I knew Britney Spears had gone straight to the hair buzzer. We'd already decided we'd take a bit more of a ceremonial approach.

Angela found *The Barber of Seville* on the salon's *Best of Italian Opera* CD and pumped up the volume.

My father closed his eyes. "Ah, Rossini," he said, as if this CD hadn't been playing practically nonstop in the salon since the 1960s.

Tulia took the scissors first. "Careful," we all said at once. Things were going so smoothly, it would be a shame to have to stop for stitches.

"Love you, Dad," she said as she made the first cut. She managed not even to nick him, which was an amazing feat for Tulia. Then she held her kids' hands while they each took a careful snip.

"Love you, Nonno," they said one by one.

"You can come to my birthday party," Maggie added when it was her turn.

Vicky started sweeping as soon as the first lock of hair fell. "Don't any of you dare throw my hair away," my father said. "I want that buried with me. It's how they do it in Italy."

"I think you mean Egypt," I said.

His eyes were scrunched closed, awaiting the next snip, but he turned his head to follow the sound. "That'll be enough out of you, Little Miss Smarty-Pants. Who's the expert here?"

"Okay," I said. "That's how they do it in Egypt *and* Italy."

Once we'd all taken a turn with the scissors, Mario brought out the buzzer.

"Not so fast," my father said. "Which one do you have there?"

Mario turned it over in his hand so he could read the label. "Remington Titanium?"

"No way," my father said. "I want the Andis T-Edger, or we quit right here."

The new buzzer was brought in. Mario did the honors, and we all watched the rest of our father's hair drop to the floor in long, spindly strips.

Then we brought him over to the sink, and Sophia scrubbed off the Cover Your Bald Spot Instantly. We had to use some Jolen Creme Bleach to get him back to his original scalp color, but it was worth the trouble.

Tulia removed the cape, and we all stepped back to survey our work.

Sophia's mother, Linda, ran her hand across my father's scalp. "Smooth as a baby's bottom," she said. "You sure do clean up nice, Larry Shaughnessy." She was practically drooling, even though she was married to some other guy now.

"Very handsome," Todd said. "And I think you look even more Italian, Lucky, if that's humanly possible."

"Kiss-up," Mario said.

I handed my father a mirror, and he moved it around so he could see all the angles. *Abbondanza!* he said. He really did look handsome. His bone structure seemed more defined, and his crinkly hazel eyes really stood out now, too. His head had a nice shape to it, too. He was a perfect MAC NW25 from the back of his neck up to the top of his head and right on down the other side. Of course, all of my family and most of the Irish Riviera could be covered in that same pale beige.

We all reached in to rub his head for good luck, and I picked up Precious so she could get a paw in there, too. "Yay, team," Angela said. She'd clearly been driving to too many sporting events, but we went along with her anyway, since we were already in the huddle.

"*T-E-A-M*," we yelled, and then we threw our hands up in the air over Lucky Larry Shaughnessy's shiny new bald head.

There was a knock on the salon door. "Somebody get that," my father said. "It's either the pizza or the paparazzi."

"Arrivederci," my father yelled when everybody finally headed out to their cars. I stayed behind to wrap up the leftover pizza in plastic wrap. Since my father and I were the two single ones, I thought I'd divide it up, and that way we could each get another meal out of it.

My father walked into the kitchen, with Precious hard on his heels. "Ciao, Bella," he said. He leaned over and kissed me on the cheek.

I rubbed his head again for good luck. I could certainly use it. "It really looks great, Dad," I said.

"I should have thought of it years ago," my father said. I could tell the story was already morphing in his mind. Before long, he'd really believe the whole thing had been his idea.

My father reached past me to open the refrigerator. "Come, Bella. Sit for a minute and share a *digestivo* with your *babbo.*"

"Oh, no," I said. "Not the grappa. You know I hate that stuff."

"Bella, Bella," he said as he pulled out the bottle anyway. "What kind of an Italian are you?"

I grabbed the refrigerator door from him and reached inside to put the pizza on the shelf. "The Irish kind? Come on, you must have something to drink in here that doesn't taste like Karo syrup." I moved things around until I found a bottle of pinot grigio. "Okay if I open this?"

My father nodded, so I went hunting for the corkscrew. My father had been divorced from his third wife for years, and his kitchen drawers had taken on a life of their own. I pulled out three golf tees and a deck of playing cards from the silverware drawer before I found the corkscrew. A long-forgotten cork was still impaled on it.

My father opened a cabinet and handed me a wineglass. As I reached for it, I saw a whole row of unopened grappa bottles lined up like soldiers across the shelf below.

"Dad," I said. "Where'd you get all that grappa?"

My father poured some grappa into an aperitif glass. He turned to admire his reflection in the glass panels of the kitchen cabinets and ran his hand over his head. "I just told those condo barracudas on the telephone that if they wanted a shot at my waterfront property, they had to sweeten the deal."

"You're not really thinking about selling, are you?" I couldn't imagine life without this house, the flagship salon attached to it.

"Nah, but it's a great way to get grappa."

"Be careful," I said. It seemed like developers were buying up the whole town. "Don't sign anything without your reading glasses, whatever you do."

My father disappeared into the living room, and *The Marriage of Figaro* blasted out. He came back in and headed over to sit at the kitchen table.

I joined him. I loved this table. It was an old pine trestle table we'd carved up pretty thoroughly over the years. It started when we were doing our homework and accidentally pressed down too hard with our pencils. We'd lift up our math sheet and $12 \div 3 = 4$ would be permanently etched below.

We began doing it on purpose after our mother moved out, throwing us into a flurry of limit testing. I remembered my father handing me a piece of sandpaper to sand off the I HATE YOU I'd carved. Angela was the one to rat me out, but I no longer remembered whether the sentiment was directed at Tulia's or Sophia's mother.

My father held up his glass. *"Salute,"* he said. *"Cin cin."*

I touched my glass to his. "What's the one Grandpa used to say?" I asked.

"Slainté," my father said.

"Slainté," I repeated as I clinked my glass to his. "I remember now. I used to think he was saying 'it's a lawn chair,' really fast." I took a sip. "You know, sometimes I wish you'd brought us up Irish instead of Italian. Life would have been simpler."

My father took a sip of his grappa. He made a face, then chugged it down. "Life is never simple," he said.

"What, you don't like grappa either?" I asked.

"The kind you get over here is too sweet

for my taste. It's much more fiery in Italy. But I still like the idea of it."

My father leaned back in his chair and clasped his hands behind his head, then ran them up and down his smooth scalp. "I suppose it's all perspective. If we were Italians living in the North End, I might have thought the Irish were the exotic ones. Your grandfather's favorite expression was 'If you're lucky enough to be Irish, you're lucky enough.' Truth be told, my father was a two-bit Irish barber, and I wanted something better for my family. It's every immigrant's dream."

I'd heard this one at least a thousand times. The real truth was that my father had been born in South Boston, so he wasn't technically an immigrant, but I took another sip of wine and let him have his version. I wondered what my dream should be, as the daughter of the son of an immigrant. Did that make me an immigrant twice removed? I'd never been able to figure out that family tree stuff. Precious jumped up on my lap, circled around, and made herself comfortable.

I didn't really plan on saying it, but it came out anyway. "Do you think it's my fault Sophia turned out the way she did?" I asked.

"What? What way did she turn out?" My father got up to ditch his grappa glass and pour a glass of pinot grigio for himself.

"I don't know," I said. "I guess I was thinking she never developed her own interests. . . ."

He topped off the wine in my glass. "And so she got interested in your husband?"

"Thanks. I don't know. Maybe it's crazy. Or maybe it's true."

My father looked up at the ceiling and took a deep breath. "And I guess I was thinking maybe you would have picked a different kind of husband if I'd set a better example."

I reached out and put my hand on his. "Oh, Dad, no. There's no connection at all."

"And you're not responsible for your sister's behavior."

"Half sister," I said.

"Blood is thicker than everything."

"Even grappa?" I took a sip of my wine, and Precious started twitching in her sleep. She was probably having a nightmare about her former owner, that awful Silly Siren bride. "You know," I said. "The thing is, I miss Sophia so much more than I ever missed Craig. But I don't see how we'll ever get past it. It's just too big a betrayal."

"L'amore domina senza regole," my father said.

"What's that?"

"Love rules without rules. At least I think that's how it translates." He grinned. "Either that or I just swore at you in Italian."

"So what's it mean? Assuming you got it right, that is."

He leaned his elbows on the table. "Everybody does stupid things in life, Bella. Some of us more than others. You think you're going to get away with it. Or they think they're going to get away with it. Or one or both of you just stop thinking. But it happens. And when it does, you can keep drinking it like poison, or you can put it behind you and go make the most of the rest of your life."

"Is that what you did with Mom?" I asked.

"No," my father said. "That's what she did with me."

14

I rifled through my lipstick drawer, looking for something strong, confident, and hydrating. Beeswax, shea butter, jojoba, and almond oil are all great moisturizing ingredients. I found a tube of Tarte Inside Out Vitamin Lipstick in a deep rose called Revive. It had jojoba, vitamins A, C, E, and K, plus acai, green tea, and lychee extract, so I figured I was covering pretty much all the bases. Maybe if I ate the whole thing like a Popsicle, I wouldn't have to take my vitamins for a couple of months.

I'd meant to call Sean Ryan to tell him I'd meet him in Providence at the college fair. I wanted to make sure he understood this was strictly business. I was all about the kits, and the fact that he was a good-looking single guy and I'd been dumped by my husband a year ago was not going to factor into the equation at all.

Of course, I distinctly remembered him

saying something or other about not being interested in me either. But people say a lot of things, so it never hurts to be sure your message is absolutely clear. Driving my own car would create a certain professional distance for both of us.

The way I looked at it, there was a nice long low-drama life ahead for me if I could just keep things simple. One small dog, some nice scenic walks, a new creative kit-making adventure. Lots of people lived perfectly fulfilling single lives. It was such an antiquated idea that people needed to be one half of a matched set, like salt and pepper shakers. I mean, what evolved person even used salt anymore?

And I'd skip the rebound relationship, thank you very much. It was actually sort of a patronizing suggestion Sean Ryan had made, if I stopped to think about it. As if I needed to have a meltdown and run around like a wronged woman for a specified period of time before I could behave myself again. Ha. Other than hitting Craig's windshield with my shoulder bag, throwing one tiny rock, and okay, putting his jock itch cream in an envelope and mailing it to Sophia, and that was ages ago, I hadn't felt the urge to act out much at all.

Sure, I'd had a few destructive fantasies.

I'd thought about strapping our mattress to the top of my Volkswagen bug and driving it into Boston, and then torching it on the street outside Craig's office. But traffic was a nightmare on the Southeast Expressway, and you'd really be taking your life in your hands trying to drive with a mattress. Plus, I didn't think Craig and Sophia had actually slept in that bed anyway. Why would they, when Sophia had a perfectly good bed of her own and no one sharing it since she'd broken up with what's his name. Sophia's boyfriends never lasted too long. I used to wonder what she was looking for. Now I knew: my husband.

So I settled for donating all our sheets, along with some of our wedding presents I'd never really liked anyway, to a women's shelter and buying new ones. Fairly pitiful as an acting-out gesture, I knew, but maybe it just meant I was a quick healer. I was calm. I was clear. I was starting to pick up the pieces of my life. I was getting ready to fly solo.

Or almost solo. Precious came skidding into the kitchen. She was wearing her DON'T HATE ME BECAUSE I'M BEAUTIFUL T-shirt today, and the soft yellow worked really well with her new highlights.

As soon as she looked up at me with her

big Chihuahua-terrier eyes, I knew she knew.

I reached down to scratch her behind one of her ears. "I'm sorry," I said. "But I really can't take you with me today. It's business."

She tilted her head and leaned into my hand as I scratched her.

"And I can't drop you off anywhere because I don't want my family to know about the kits. You have no idea how controlling they can be, and five will get you ten, they'll try to get in on the action. So it's better just to keep my mouth shut, you know?"

Precious raised her tufted eyebrows. This talking-to-your-dog thing was really addictive. I wondered if it would be completely rude to call Sean Ryan now and tell him I'd meet him there. Of course, I'd have to get directions, since so far I only knew we were going somewhere in Providence, which was a pretty big city. Maybe I could follow him. I'd just tell him I had something to do afterward, and there was no sense driving all the way back here to get my car.

It sounded like a plan. I'd packed all the kits I'd made into two big cardboard boxes before I went to bed last night, so I piled one on top of the other, swung my bag over my shoulder, got my keys ready in one hand. I opened the door a crack and threw a dog treat way across the room for Precious to chase.

"I'll be back soon," I said matter-of-factly. I wondered how people ever managed to leave actual children. I picked up the boxes and started backing my way calmly out the door.

I pulled the door shut and leaned the boxes against the doorframe while I locked it. I turned around and took a step. Precious yelped.

I screamed. "Ohmigod, are you okay? How did you get out here anyway?"

I heard a car door slam. "Are you talking to yourself up there?" Sean Ryan yelled.

I looked down over the railing. "Nope. I'm just being outsmarted by a small dog. Do you think I can get away with bringing her?"

He smiled up at me. He was wearing dark jeans and a navy-and-white-striped shirt with the sleeves rolled up. It was a good thing he answered, because I'd forgotten the question. "Why not?" he said. "She can be our chaperone."

I opened my mouth to tell him we wouldn't be needing one.

"I know," he said. "We won't be needing one."

"Exactly," I said.

"Exactly," he said. "So, she can be our assistant." He ran up the steps two at a time and grabbed the boxes out of my hands.

He was already halfway down the stairs before I thought of it. "I can get those," I yelled in the direction of his back. I bent down and picked up Precious. "Guess he has them," I said.

I unlocked my door again, then ran back in and grabbed some dog food and a few of Precious's favorite toys. By the time Precious and I caught up to Sean Ryan, he was already putting the boxes in the trunk of his dark green Prius. "Um," I said.

He shut the trunk and turned to face me. "Um?" he said.

I didn't remember him being quite so good-looking. "Maybe I should take my car? You know, just in case you have plans? No, that's not it. I mean, I have plans. Oh, forget it." Precious and I walked around to the passenger side.

"Are you okay?" he asked as we were buckling our seat belts.

"Fine," I said. "So, how many miles do you *really* get to the gallon in this thing?" It seemed to me that the interior could have been bigger. When I'd reached for my seat belt, our knuckles had almost brushed.

"Who knows. But it sure makes me feel

superior." Precious jumped over onto his lap. I certainly wasn't planning on reaching for her, that was for sure, so she was going to have to find her own way back.

"What?" I said.

"I was kidding," he said. "You didn't smile." He handed Precious back to me and this time our hands did touch for an instant.

I pulled my hand away. "I guess it wasn't that funny," I said.

He started the car. "Consider the bar raised," he said. He backed out of the parking lot and took a right toward the highway. "Are you sure you're okay?"

"Couldn't be better," I said. I smoothed out my pants and adjusted the summer-weight Chico's jacket I was wearing so it wouldn't get mangled by the seat belt. "So how much do I owe you for the right half of the display table today?"

"You can buy dinner," he said.

I clapped my hands together. It made a bigger noise than I would have imagined, and Precious jumped between the seats and into the back. "Listen," I said. "Just in case you've forgotten, this is strictly business."

"Okay," he said. "We can split the tab. But I'm only paying for the things I order, so if you order an appetizer and I don't, I don't want to hear any whining when we tally up."

"Don't be so irrelevant," I said.

"Katharine Hepburn to Cary Grant, *Bringing Up Baby,* 1938."

I turned to look at him. *"What?"*

"It's a line in the movie. Or pretty close to it. And I think right after that Cary Grant says something about being strangely drawn to her in moments of quiet."

"Are you telling me to shut up?"

He laughed. He had a nice full laugh, nothing held back, right out there for the whole world to hear. I would have probably liked it a lot better if it hadn't been directed at me.

He took the same back roads out to the highway I would have taken. Maybe we'd been passing each other on this route for years. I was an intelligent woman, but my brain seemed temporarily to have shut down. We'd made it out to the highway already, and Sean Ryan put on his blinker and got ready to merge onto the highway. He accelerated, and we blended seamlessly into the traffic. "So, what's your all-time favorite old movie?" he asked.

"Hmm," I said. "Lately I guess it's been *Thelma and Louise.*" I didn't think it was necessary to tell him I'd watched it three times just this past week and that one of those times I got a little bit carried away and kept rewinding and replaying the shooting scene, just so I could pretend the guy was Craig. "I mean, they got a life, they kicked butt. Okay, so they died in the end, but doesn't everybody?"

Sean Ryan nodded. "God, I remember my wife dragging me kicking and screaming to that one. It was a great road movie though. She wasn't often right like that."

I turned to see if he was smiling. He looked at me at the same time. "My husband wasn't often right either," I said.

"I bet not being often right is the one thing all exes have in common."

I nodded. Neither of us said anything for a while. Precious found her way back to my lap again, and I looked out the window while I stroked her wiry fur.

"So how much longer do you get to keep the dog?" Sean Ryan asked.

I whipped my head around to face him. "What do you mean by *that?*"

"What do I mean by *what?* You have to give it back, right?"

"I don't know," I said. "I think if they wanted her, they would have come to get her by now, don't you?"

"Wow," he said. "You've got a real talent for denial, don't you?"

162

15

As soon as Sean Ryan asked me about giving Precious back, it hit me like a ton of bricks that she'd found her way into my heart, and I couldn't imagine my life without her. Why is it that even when you're trying your hardest not to get attached, something still sneaks up on you? I'd make a lousy Buddhist. I'd probably spend all day trying to build a perfect sandcastle, and then when the tide turned and it was time to let the waves crash it to smithereens to remind me of life's impermanence, I'd dig it up fast and find a way to carry it home.

But, I mean, stupid as it sounded, I'd lost Sophia. I'd lost Craig. I couldn't even think about losing this sweet little dog, too. We'd just pulled into the North Garage at the Rhode Island Convention Center, and I was trying really hard not to cry. I never cried, but at this moment it felt like Precious was all I really had.

Sean Ryan found a space near an entrance and put the car into park. "Hey," he said. "I'm really sorry I said that. It came out a lot harsher than I meant it to. I mean, maybe they'll just let you keep the dog."

I took a quick wipe at one of my eyes with the back of my hand. "Well, it sounds pretty silly when you say it that way. I don't know. I keep thinking maybe they've forgotten about her. Newlyweds have a lot going on, you know?"

"How long has it been? About a week, right?"

"No," I said. "I think it's been much longer than that." I closed my eyes and made myself do the math in my head. "Ohmigod. You're right. A week. Today. You don't remember how long honeymoons last, do you?"

"Never long enough," Sean Ryan said.

I picked up Precious and rested her against my shoulder while I patted her back. "It's just that the bride who owned her didn't even like her." I covered one of Precious's ears with my hand and pressed her other ear into my neck. "I distinctly remember her saying next time she was getting a *Peekapoo*," I whispered.

"Did you just cover its ears when you said that?"

"What? She doesn't miss a trick."

Sean Ryan looked at his watch. "Listen," he said. "It's getting close to noon. We'd better get inside. But don't worry, there's got to be a way to keep it. Let's both think on it, and we'll come up with a plan over dinner."

"Thanks," I said. "But she's not an it. She's a she."

Sean Ryan reached over and gave Precious a pat. "Sorry, girl," he said. He rested his hand on my shoulder, and for a moment, I thought he might hug me. I could almost feel his crisp, striped shirt against my skin.

He opened his car door, and I watched his shirt disappear. I got out, too, and we went around to the back of the Prius and started unloading our boxes.

I kept Precious safely in my bag while we showed our driver's licenses at a table in the lobby. A frazzled woman handed us our badges, and we headed for the escalator.

Our table turned out to be in the Rotunda Room, which was nice and sunny, and Sean Ryan let me have the right side without a fight. Tweedy people were shuffling around everywhere, getting things set up. I didn't see any makeup people, but there were massage tables set up at the other end of the room. I wondered if the safe sumo wrestling ring was around here somewhere, too.

Sean Ryan covered our table with a white tablecloth, then unloaded his college kits. He nodded at my boxes. "Okay," he said. "Show me what you've got."

I put my shoulder bag on the floor, and Precious poked her head out and looked around. She seemed fine, so I opened up one of my boxes and started pulling out my kits.

"Hey," Sean Ryan said. "Those are great. Where did you find them?"

"I made them. Or at least I decorated them."

I couldn't imagine how people managed to survive in parts of the country where they don't have Christmas Tree Shops. The Christmas part is the least of it. They have just so many bargains, so many things you have no idea you need until you see them and you suddenly can't live without them. And it's all dirt cheap.

Earlier in the week I'd gone to the one in Marshbury and found clear plastic toiletry travel cases with little pockets in the front. I'd filled the pockets with tiny cutout foam shapes — flowers, faces, yin-yang symbols, and *B*s for *Bella* — and then sealed them shut with my hot glue gun. When you shook the bag, the shapes moved around. It was

166

kind of like a beauty snow globe.

Then I tied a strip of raffia through the zipper pull and tied a tag onto that. I'd made the tags by cutting pieces of mulberry paper with grasslike strands in it and punching holes in them. Then I hand painted them in my signature calligraphylike lettering, the same kind I used anytime one of the salons needed a sign. Every once in a while having gone to art school actually came in handy.

I'd struggled with a name for the kits. Bella's Beauty Bag? Beauty Bag by Bella? Bella's Bag? Beauty by Bella? Finally, I'd settled on Bella's Bag of Beauty Basics. Now I wasn't so sure.

Sean Ryan turned one over in his hand. "Wow," he said. "You have a great eye for packaging. It's so simple, but really effective. What did these case things cost?"

I wondered if I should tell the truth. Maybe it was a trick question. "Three for five dollars?" I said. "Plus a dollar sixty-nine a package for each of the cutouts, but I still have some left."

"That's amazing." He shook his head. "How many did you buy? And can you get more?"

"I bought ninety-three, which was all they had. I figured I could always return them.

And, sure, I can get more. I'd just have to drive around to all the other Christmas Tree Shops."

He nodded at the college kits. "I don't even want to tell you how much I paid to have these boxes done. But what happens if you run out of Christmas Tree Shops?"

"I guess I'd just discontinue this case and find something else."

"Makes sense to me." He looked at his watch. "Okay, the doors are about to open. You handle your kit the way you want to, of course, but what I'm doing is simple. I count the number of kits I give away. I take notes about the comments I receive. I get everybody's e-mail addresses so I can get feedback from them after they use it, since most of them will never send in the comment card. I'm essentially trying to build a case so I can help my friend sell the kit to one of the college testing companies, or even the right publisher."

He actually sounded like he knew what he was talking about, but I still had one big question. "So, do you get a flat rate for doing this, or do you take a percentage?"

College students and their parents suddenly started stampeding into the Rotunda Room. The noise was deafening. "Just helping out a friend," Sean Ryan had to practically yell, even though he was right next to me.

Precious jumped up on my lap. "I hope that guidance counselor appreciates you," I yelled back.

Makeup is practically irresistible to almost everyone. That's because it's optimism in a bottle. The college kids and their mothers stood spellbound while I filled out their diagrams to show them how and where to apply their makeup.

"Gee," the kids said, "I had no idea you were supposed to powder your eyes before you apply the shadow."

"Absolutely," I said. "It helps it to stick."

"Why do you put the blush up that high?" their mothers asked.

"Because," I said, "if it drops below the apple of your cheek, it'll make your face look saggy."

Then I made notes with product suggestions in the margins. And after that I'd start mixing up their customized foundation. "Wow," the kids said. "Nicole had this done. I think I read about it in some magazine."

"I bet she paid more than twenty-nine ninety-five," their mothers said.

"Probably more like ten thousand," I said, then I looked up to watch their jaws drop.

I'd actually read about celebrities paying this much for custom makeup in Paris. Talk about money to burn, even if you factored in the poor exchange rate with the euro. I mean, what could the ingredients in that foundation possibly be? Bovine collagen from firstborn free-range yak virgins?

I finished mixing their foundation with my little white disposable spatula, then I handed them a mirror and pointed. "Always test the foundation at your jawline. Right there. If the foundation is the right shade, it'll disappear into your skin and you won't see a line at all."

Then I took a triangular foam sponge from the pack and did a quick makeup application. The kids and their mothers followed along on the diagram, like they were studying for a test.

The mothers were the first to snap out of it. "College," they said. "We're here to find a college."

"Have you started your applications?" I asked sweetly.

The daughters looked away. The mothers got a look of grim determination in their eyes.

Then I reached over and grabbed one of the college application kits from Sean Ryan's rapidly diminishing pile. "Here you go," I said. "I'll even save you from having to go over and stand in that long line over there. Just write down your e mail address and zip code for the nice man over there. You'll breeze right through your college applications with this."

"Did your kids use it?" one of the mothers asked.

"Absolutely," I said. "All five of them loved it."

When she walked away, I thought about Lizzie. I wondered if I should call her to say I was waiting for her father to call. I wondered if Craig would actually call. I wondered if there was a way to get out of talking to Craig that would still let me get Lizzie back into my life.

It was a long, grueling couple of hours, but Sean Ryan and I managed to survive the entire fair, which felt like a cross between a circus and a root canal without the drugs. I got up and stretched, then started counting my used makeup sponges.

"So, once again, we missed the sumo wrestling," Sean Ryan said. "I can't tell you how disappointed I am." He walked around to the front of my end of the table and pointed at a guy in white diapers coming out of the men's room.

"I don't get it," I said. "Why did he need

the men's room if he's wearing a diaper? It's redundant." I put the sponges back on the table again. "Damn, now you made me forget what number I was on." I started picking up sponges again as I counted.

"Why are you counting used sponges?"

I threw the sponges back on the table. "If you must know, I'm trying to see how much I suffered, and you're certainly not making it any easier."

I looked up so I could glare at him. He smiled. "Did anybody ever tell you what a sunny disposition you have?"

"Yeah," I said. "All the time."

"Great," he said. "Maybe it'll turn into a self-fulfilling prophecy." Precious jumped up on the table, and Sean Ryan picked her up. "Listen, just in case it's helpful, you might want to compare the ratio of the number of makeup applications you did to the number of kits you sold."

"Oh, please," I said. "As if I was going to do their makeup if they didn't buy a kit."

16

We didn't know of any dog-friendly restaurants in Rhode Island, so we decided to get the drive out of the way and then pick up fish and chips in Marshbury to eat at the beach. I counted my cash while Sean Ryan drove the Prius north on 95. I had well over a thousand dollars in my hot little hands.

"You can order whatever you want," I said. I arranged all the bills from smallest to largest, and made sure all the dead presidents' heads were facing the same way. I always did this with my tips, too. There's nothing more soothing than a well-organized pile of cash.

Sean Ryan smiled. "Be careful," he said. "I'm liable to order the french fries *and* the onion rings."

"They're your arteries."

"Good strategy. Maybe I'll just watch you eat."

I folded over the wad of bills, wrapped a

hair elastic around it, and buried it in the bottom of my shoulder bag. "So," I said, "you're not really test marketing the guidance counselor's kit for free, are you? I mean, don't you have to make a living? Even with the gas mileage you get on your Prius?"

Sean Ryan looked over briefly, then put his eyes right back on the road. He was a good driver, steady and confident without being show-offy. "Don't worry, I have some other things going on. I have lots of irons in the fire, different projects at various stages."

"So, what, you're an entrepreneur?"

"Yeah, essentially. I think the dictionary definition is a risk-taking businessman who sets up and finances new commercial enterprises to make a profit." He put on his blinker and moved into the passing lane. "I like to start things, and then I like to get rid of them before they get boring."

"How many times did you say you've been married again?"

Sean Ryan laughed that big laugh of his again. "Just once. But I have to tell you my wife hated it when I left my corporate marketing job and went out on my own. I felt free as a bird, but she was terrified of the risk. And she missed the pension plan. I started a SEP-IRA, but it just wasn't the same for her." He looked over at me again.

"A joke," he said.

"Cute," I said. "So what other kinds of projects are you involved in?"

"A small brewery that's working on making a beer with as many antioxidants as red wine."

"Is that possible?"

"Sure. Right now a nice high-end beer contains more than twice the antioxidants of white wine, and half that of red. But there's some evidence that the large antioxidant molecules found in red wine may be less readily absorbed by the body than the smaller molecules found in beer. So, if we can up the antioxidant level at the same time we buzz the absorption issue . . ."

I looked at him. "Buzz the absorption issue?"

He shrugged. "You asked. Also, I invest in property development, mostly waterfront condos."

"My father would call you a barracuda," I said.

"Yeah, well, the way I look at it, they're going to happen with or without me, and I can help keep them green and aesthetically pleasing. Anyway, I'm also involved in a couple of microfinance projects in developing countries. You know, a group gets together to help create and consolidate local financial structures to manage loans and savings —"

"Oh, that," I said. "I was just talking to some friends about getting one of those together." I looked over at him. "A joke," I said.

Sean Ryan cleared his throat. "We also facilitate access to technical advice to improve local income-generating activities, things like agriculture, livestock, and fishery production. It's really interesting stuff. And it's nice to feel like you're helping people who need it."

"Is that how you pick your projects?"

"Sometimes. And sometimes I pick them so I can eat."

"Or so a guidance counselor with a dream can eat?"

Sean Ryan shrugged. "I'll take the kits to a college fair in Atlanta next weekend, then I'll help him pull all the feedback together."

"Did you just say you're going to be in Atlanta next weekend?"

"Yeah, why?"

"Me, too. My nephew's getting married at the Margaret Mitchell House."

"Will you get to watch *Gone With the Wind*?"

"Not very original." I shook my head. "You know, I've never been to a Southern wedding, but I'm a little bit afraid they're going to serve okra."

"Okraphobic, huh? Well, get ready, it's in season from May through October. Actually, it's not bad. And it's high in fiber, calcium, and folic acid."

"I'll take your word for it," I said.

Sean Ryan smiled. "Anyway, if you feel like fitting in a college fair first, feel free to use half of my table again. But I call the right side this time."

"Sure," I said. A few hours at a college fair would pay for my whole weekend, including hotel and airfare. But what I was really thinking about was how much easier it would be to handle a wedding that my half sister would most likely be attending with my ex-husband if I had a date. Not a date date, of course. Just someone to make me look a little less conspicuously single. "I know," I said. "How about I go to the college fair with you, and then you can come to my nephew's wedding with me?"

Sean Ryan grinned. "Why, Bella Shaughnessy, you're not asking me out on a date, are you?"

"Don't be ridiculous," I said. "I just want you there to eat my okra."

It was a perfect late summer night to sit on

the beach and eat fish and chips. I'd packed a little can of dog food for Precious, since I didn't know how long we'd be gone. I pulled off the flip top and set it down on the sand, and she began eating daintily from the can. I could tell she would have preferred a nice bowl, but she was being a good sport about it.

"Well," Sean Ryan said. "One week later and here we are again. You know, I'm starting to think of this as our beach."

I opened my mouth, then closed it again when I saw he was smiling. "Cute," I said.

A seagull flew just overhead, assessing its chances for a french fry. "Don't even think about it," I yelled. The seagull turned and headed out over the ocean.

Sean Ryan raised an eyebrow. "So, what, now you're talking back to seagulls?"

"It worked, didn't it? If the tourists would just stop feeding them and turning them into beach pigeons . . ."

"Beach pigeons," he said. "I like that. It has a nice ring to it." He stabbed at his fish with a plastic fork, and the fork snapped in half.

I laughed.

"Thanks," he said. He reached for the fish with his fingers and broke off a piece and popped it into his mouth. "It tastes better like this anyway."

I ditched my fork, too, and ate a piece of fish with my fingers. "You're right," I said.

"That's a first," he said. "Not that I'm counting. Okay, let's talk about the dog. I think the first thing you need to do is look into the laws about lost-and-found pets."

Precious had finished her meal and was whipping a piece of seaweed around down by the water. "I disagree," I said. "I think the first thing we need to do is disguise her."

"Okay," he said. "And how might *we* do that?"

I took another bite of fish, then closed the Styrofoam takeout container. "Come on," I said. "We can finish these at Salon de Paolo."

Sean Ryan was using the salon computer to search the Internet, and I was mixing up some Aveda Full Spectrum Protective Permanent Crème Hair Color. It was the darkest color they made, Level 1, which was a blue black, what I thought of as coal black. Far too many older women picked a dark, shoe polishy color like this, hoping to return to the deep color of their youth, and they never even noticed it was so harsh it washed out their coloring and called attention to each and every wrinkle. Women's hair color should always go lighter as they age.

But Level 1 was a great color for a dog, and this particular product was 97 percent natural and fairly gentle for a permanent color. I was a little bit concerned about using it so soon after those highlights, but desperate times called for desperate measures.

I screwed the top on the applicator bottle and started shaking it. I loved being in the salon after hours. It reminded me of when we were little kids, and we'd get to hang out with my father while my mother cooked a big Sunday dinner, and he caught up on work. He'd pull out some bins filled to the brim with pink rollers and silver hair clips for us, and Angela, Mario, and I would go to town on our dolls.

We'd start by washing their hair in the sinks. I had a Tressy doll. She had a tiny key that was attached to a white belt wrapped around her waist. You inserted the key in her back, very *Stepford Wives* in hindsight, and I remembered wondering if it hurt her. You twisted the key to make her hair shorter, but before I washed Tressy, I'd push the button in her tummy and yank on the hair to make it as long as it would go.

Angela had a Cricket doll, who was Tressy's little sister, just like Angela was mine. Cricket also had hair that grew and a key hanging from a belt. Mario had started out with a G.I. Joe, but he'd lobbied long and hard until eventually he got his own Mary Make Up. Mary's hair didn't grow, but her face was waxy, so that makeup could be applied to it and easily removed.

Mario took to her like a duck to water, and it was no surprise to anyone that the trajectory of his life had gone from Mary Make Up to professional hair and makeup. Mary Make Up and Tressy were exactly the same size, and Mario and I loved that we could share clothes and have twice the wardrobe.

After we washed the dolls' hair, we'd pile boxes on salon chairs so the dolls could sit high enough for us to work on them, and then we'd start wrapping their hair around the smallest curlers we could find. We taught ourselves to make spit curls, too, with real spit, and to anchor them with silver hair clips. Then we'd hold the dolls under the hair dryers, checking them occasionally to make sure they didn't start to melt.

"Listen to this," Sean Ryan said. "I think I've got something. It's a Massachusetts statute. 'Public Safety and Good Order, Chapter One Thirty-four, Lost Goods and Stray Beasts.' "

"Did you hear that, honey?" I said to Precious. "He called you a beast." Precious gave me a look that could only be described as proud, then she jumped up on Sean Ryan's lap.

He reached one hand down to pet her. "Okay, it says that any person who takes up a stray beast shall report, post, or advertise the finding thereof, giving a description of the color and the natural and artificial marks of such beast, otherwise he shall not be entitled to compensation for any expenses which he may incur relative thereto."

"Come on, in English, please."

"Okay, wait." We waited while Sean Ryan read through the legalese. "This doesn't really apply. It's more about the fact that you can auction off the beast after three months, and if the owner shows up within a year, you get to deduct your caring-for-the-beast expenses before you split the profits from the auction with the owner."

"That's awful," I said. "It makes them sound like cattle or something."

"I think they are talking about cattle," Sean Ryan said. "Wait, here's something else on another link. Okay, it says that the question of lost-and-found pets does not have an easy legal answer."

"Duh," I said.

He smiled and brushed some hair off his forehead. "Okay, the common law that has developed through court decisions generally holds that the person who can assert true ownership has superior rights. The court may consider other factors, however, such as how long the person who found a dog has cared for it . . ."

"A week is nothing to sneeze at," I said.

". . . how much effort has been made by the original owner to find it . . ."

I shook my head. "Like, none."

". . . and the relative value each party has invested in the pet in terms of care."

I walked over and picked up Precious. "Okay, enough with the computer," I said to Sean Ryan. "We're about to give this beast a new identity."

17

"Here," I said. "Put these latex gloves on."

Sean Ryan raised an eyebrow. He'd already rolled up his sleeves a little bit higher, and I'd draped a black cape with SALON DE PAOLO printed in gold over him.

"Just do it. Otherwise your hands will get dyed, too."

"Ohh-kay," he said slowly. He took the gloves from me and pulled at one of them, then let it go with a snap.

"*What* are you doing?"

"I've always wanted to try that. Like on one of those TV medical shows."

I gave the hair color another shake. "Come on, we don't have time to fool around. Your job is to keep her from licking it off. Just get a good hold on her, but try not to rub off any of the dye."

"Great," Sean Ryan said. He started to put one hand into a glove, but his fingers got stuck halfway.

I put the hair color down and pulled the glove off him. I held it to my mouth like a balloon and blew into it. When the fingers of the glove grew about two sizes, I handed it back to Sean Ryan.

"Wow," he said. "You must be a big hit at birthday parties. Can you make those balloon animals?"

I ignored him and blew up his other glove. I handed it to him, then I picked up Precious and put her on the tabletop at my station. She looked up at me calmly.

"Approximately how long are we talking about here?" he asked.

"Well, it's hard to say. Her hair's pretty coarse, which might make it resistant, but she's also had a recent process, which might make it absorb more quickly."

"In English, please."

"I don't know," I said. "I'll start checking after thirty minutes, but it could take up to forty. We want to make sure she looks like a true brunette."

"Oh, boy," he said.

I started at her hind legs and worked my way forward. The long point of the applicator bottle made it just as easy to dye a dog as a person. I'd make a part in the fur and run a line of color almost at the skin line, then I'd work it out to the end, using my glove-covered fingers to make sure I didn't miss a spot. I'd been doing this since high school, so I was both speedy and efficient.

About halfway through, Precious started to shake, which hardly ever happened with humans. Dye drops flew everywhere.

"Do something," I yelled.

Sean Ryan let go with one hand to wipe at a spot of black dye on his cheek, which only created a long dark smear. "Sure," he said. "Any suggestions?"

"Just try to hold her still," I said. "I'll go as fast as I can."

I finally finished. Sean Ryan took a deep breath. "Now what?" he asked.

"Now you keep holding her, and I'll get the dye off your face before it's permanent."

When I came back with a cotton ball and a bottle of Clean Touch color remover for skin, Sean Ryan was holding Precious behind her front legs and singing "Ninety-Nine Bottles of Beer on the Wall" to her.

"That's the spirit," I said. I soaked the cotton ball and reached for his face.

He stopped singing. "What is that stuff? Not that I don't trust you, of course."

Precious got ready to shake. "Don't stop," I said.

"Take one down," he sang. He had a nice strong baritone, although he might have been a tiny bit flat.

"It's only color remover." I dabbed at a spot on his nose. "My father says they used to use cigarette ashes for this, but that's not very PC these days. Toothpaste works pretty well, too."

"Pass it around," Sean Ryan sang. He stopped singing long enough to say, "Fascinating," then segued right into, "ninety-seven bottles of beer on the wall."

"I can't believe I made it all the way to thirty-seven bottles," Sean Ryan said. He was spinning himself around in one of the salon chairs. "I think you should have had to sing, too."

"That's because you haven't heard my voice."

"Well, you owe me. Big-time. First me giving you the right half of the table, then holding down your dog for you. . . ."

I finished towel drying Precious and put her back on the tabletop. "So, send me a bill."

He stopped spinning and looked at me in the mirror. "That's okay. I'll take it out in trade. After you finish the dog, you can give me a makeover. I'll want to look my best for that wedding."

"Here," I said. "Keep an eye on her for a

minute." As soon as Sean Ryan had his hands on Precious, I walked into the other room, flicked a switch on the wax machine, and came right back.

"What was that all about?" he asked.

"Nothing," I said. "I just remembered something." I picked up the Andis T-Edger, the same buzzer we'd used on my father, and snapped on a number three guard. "Okay, break time's over. I need you to hold her again."

Sean Ryan pushed himself out of his chair and got a good grip on Precious, and I started buzzing off her fur to a nice crew cut length.

"Don't forget." He was yelling so I could hear him over the sound of the buzzer. "She still needs a new name."

"What about Priceless?"

He shook his head. "Too close to Precious. What about P? You know, like P Diddy? Maybe P Puppy?"

"Nah," I said. I turned off the buzzer so I could take a look at my progress. "What about Lucy? I always wanted to be named Lucy."

Sean Ryan let go and walked over to the other side of the salon and squatted down. "Here, Lucy," he called.

Precious ignored him and looked at me.

"I rest my case," Sean Ryan said.

He came over to hold her again, and I finished the buzz cut. Then I got out my scissors to trim off her tufted eyebrows. Since they were one of her best features, this was a little bit sad, but necessary.

I took a step back to get a better look. "Holy cannoli," I said. "She's a whole new beast."

"That's it," Sean Ryan said.

"What's it?" I said.

He walked back over to the other side of the room and squatted down again. "Here, Cannoli," he called.

Precious ran over to him and licked his face.

"No way," I said. "Anything but Cannoli. Plus, I think it's more of a blond name than a brunette name."

Sean Ryan walked across the salon and squatted down again. "Cannoli," he sang.

Precious ran right over to him.

"It's perfect," he said. He looked around the salon. Although Salon de Paolo didn't have a kiddie area with a fake Tuscan wall like Salon de Lucio, it did have Corinthian columns flanking the door on the inside, plus a two-tiered fountain next to the reception desk. "It's like she joined a witness protection program and was given a whole new identity. She'll fit right in."

I had to admit there was a certain logic to this, but I wasn't completely convinced. "I don't know, I think we might have enough fake Italians running around this place. Maybe we should broaden our horizons and call her Croissant. I could buy her a little pink beret."

Sean Ryan shook his head. "Cannoli," he said. "It's a done deal. Okay, moving on."

"Boy, it sure didn't take you long to start getting bossy." I patted the chair in front of me. "Next," I said.

"I think I might have only been kidding about that makeover," he said.

"Too late," I said.

He sat. I opened my razor. He opened his eyes wide. "You're scaring me," he said.

"You'll barely feel a thing," I said, just so I could watch him cringe some more. I started razoring. "I'm not going to touch the length much at all, but it'll look a lot better and be much easier for you to manage if we take out some of the bulk."

Sean Ryan met my eyes in the mirror. "Is that the first thing you thought of when you saw me? I mean, have you been plotting to take away some of my bulk since the day we met?"

"Shh," I said. I kept razoring, staying loose

and working with his hair so the best shape could emerge. A great haircut is like a work of art, and like all true artists, the best stylists know enough to relax and go with the flow. You're trying to find the essence of your subject and elevate it to a whole new level. I mean, art is art, and I felt like if Picasso walked into the salon for a haircut, we'd really have a lot to say to each other. Unless he turned out to be a pretentious jerk, of course. Then I'd just keep my mouth shut and cut his hair.

I put my razor down and shook up a container of Paul Mitchell Extra-Body Sculpting Foam. "Okay," I said. "Just squirt about this much into your palm, rub it between your hands, and work it all the way through your hair, starting at the roots."

Sean Ryan raised an eyebrow. "I'm not a Neanderthal, you know. I have used hair gunk before."

"Sor-ry," I said. I handed him the container. "Here, you can keep the rest of it."

"Thanks."

"Okay, close your eyes, and I'll be right back."

"Here, Cannoli," I called, just to practice saying it. She followed me into the treatment room, and I dipped a Popsicle stick into hot wax and jogged back to Sean Ryan so it would stay hot.

"Wow," he said. "That feels great. I've never had a facial before."

I pressed the cloth strip down and let it cool a bit, then I pulled his skin taut with one hand. "Quick like a Band Aid," I said. Then I pulled off the strip.

He yelped. "What the hell was that? And thanks for the warning, by the way."

I smiled. "Hey, you were the one who said you weren't a Neanderthal. So you shouldn't have a unibrow."

He leaned forward in the chair and squinted at himself in the mirror. "I can't believe you did that to me. And no way did I have a unibrow."

"Okay," I said. "A borderline unibrow. See how much better you look now? It really opens up your eyes."

"Wow, look how red it's getting. I hope you're happy now."

"Delirious," I said.

Everything was fine until I leaned over him to dab on some Wax Off, a gel that not only gets rid of any residual stickiness from the wax, but also soothes the skin. I was massaging it in, and suddenly he opened his eyes. We looked at each other. One of his hands somehow ended up on the small of my back.

We looked at each other some more. I knew whenever I smelled Paul Mitchell Extra-Body Sculpting Foam from then on, I'd think of him. One of my hands found its way to his shoulder.

"Hey," I said.

He put his other hand on my back. "Hey," he said.

The salon door opened, and Cannoli went crazy.

18

"I saw the light on down here and thought it might be you," Craig said. "Sophia told me you told her at your father's Salon de Lucio meeting yesterday that you wanted to talk. . . ."

Sean Ryan opened his eyes wide. "Your father owns Salon de Lucio?" he asked. Since it didn't seem like the best time to review my father's business portfolio, I just nodded.

"Oh, boy," he said.

Cannoli made a flying leap and started circling around Craig, nipping at the air around his ankles with eight pounds of pure ferocity.

"Whoa," Craig said. "Do you think you can call that thing off? What is it, anyway? A black Brillo pad?"

It probably said something about my former husband that he hadn't yet noticed that I was leaning over another man and that our arms and legs had arranged themselves a little bit like a pretzel. Interest in other people had never been his strong suit.

Sean Ryan untangled himself from me and pushed his way out of the chair. He took off his Salon de Paolo cape while I walked over to pick up Cannoli. She leaned out over my arms and snarled at Craig, exposing her tiny pointy teeth.

Craig looked past me. "Oh, sorry," he said. "I didn't realize you had a customer."

I don't know why I hesitated. I guess I was trying to figure out what to say. Should I introduce Sean Ryan as my business acquaintance? My fellow kit person? My co-dog dyer? The man who was coming to my nephew's wedding with me to make it easier to deal with the fact that you'd be there with my half sister? The guy I was just about to kiss before you so rudely interrupted us?

Sean Ryan reached into his pocket and threw some bills on my tabletop.

"Thanks for the haircut," he said as he passed me.

He walked between the Corinthian columns and out the salon door without looking back.

"So, are you going to invite me upstairs?" Craig asked. He was wearing jeans and a

T-shirt, and he looked like he could use a good night's sleep.

"Nope," I said. I kept Cannoli in my arms and walked over and sat down in the chair Sean Ryan had just vacated. It was still warm, and I took a moment to breathe in the lingering coconut smell of his Paul Mitchell Extra-Body Sculpting Foam. I was happy to see he hadn't forgotten to take the rest of it with him.

Craig shrugged and sat down in the next chair over.

"So," I said. I twisted my chair a quarter turn in his direction. "How about those Red Sox?"

"Listen," Craig said. "Let's not play games. What's this about Lizzie?"

I wanted to say, *What's what about Lizzie?* just to make him nuts, but I resisted. "She asked me to talk to you."

He glared at me. I waited.

"About *what?*" he finally had to ask.

"Don't use that tone of voice with me," I said.

"Don't make me use it then," he said.

Cannoli licked my face. I stood up. "Never mind," I said. "You can go back to your girlfriend now."

Craig leaned back in his chair and shut his eyes. "Jesus," he said. "Were you always

196

this much of a bitch?"

"I don't know," I said. "Were you always this much of an asshole?"

His eyes were still closed. He smiled. "Probably. You just didn't notice, because I was so hot."

"Oh, yeah, right. In your dreams."

He opened his eyes. They had big, not-so-hot circles under them. I couldn't for the life of me remember what I'd seen in him. I couldn't even manage to remember much about our marriage. It seemed two-dimensional in hindsight, like looking back at a series of old-fashioned black-and-white snapshots. We both worked a lot. We spent a lot of time taking care of his kids. He played a lot of golf. I hung out with my family a lot.

He told me his ex-wife was a bitch a lot, too. I wondered if she was still a bitch now that I was a bitch, or if my moving up to the title somehow debitched her. He wasn't too crazy about my family, with the exception of Sophia, notable in hindsight, and the feeling was mutual. He only remembered to bring me flowers after a fight. Had we ever been happy?

"Come on, Bella. What's going on with Lizzie?"

I put Precious, I mean Cannoli, on the

floor, and she bared her teeth at Craig, then turned her back on him and headed over to drink from the bottom tier of the fountain. We used to drink out of that fountain as kids, so I figured it was probably as safe now as it was then. "She called me," I said. "She wants to change her major to culinary arts so she can have her own show on the Food Network."

"I hope you stayed out of it," he said.

Until that very moment, I'd planned to. "What's wrong with it?" I said. "It's her life."

"She got a perfect score on her SAT subject test in chemistry."

"She did not. She got a seven twenty. And there's tons of chemistry in cooking. That's probably why she likes it so much."

Craig crossed his arms over his chest. "Some of us dream bigger than that, Bella."

"Did you think that up before or after you slept with my sister?"

Craig shut his eyes again. "Half sister. We were separated. Come on, do we have to go there again? Can't we just get past the drama and move on?"

"But how could you do that to me?" I heard myself asking, like a soap star who needed better dialogue.

"I didn't do it to you. It just happened. I

guess I just thought I'd get away with it."

I couldn't listen to this sitting down, so I jumped up. "What? What do you mean, you thought you'd get away with it? You didn't think I'd recognize you at the dinner table at Christmas?"

Craig was actually looking at me now. He ran his hands through his thinning hair and shook his head. "I guess I didn't think it would happen more than once. I don't know, I thought she'd be more like you, and not so, I don't know, clingy."

This was a whole new category of overshare. I wanted to cover my ears and close my eyes for as long as it took for Craig to go away and for me to forget what he'd just said. But I knew, no matter what I did, I'd remember this one.

"What?" I finally yelled. "You took my sister away from me and now you don't even want her?"

Things might have been different if the ceiling hadn't started dripping on Craig's head. But it did. He looked up, and a second drop landed right in his eye. I had a knee-jerk urge to laugh, and it was halfway out of my mouth before I kind of swallowed it back.

Craig wiped his eye with the back of his hand. "Geez, Bella, you didn't leave the toilet running, did you?"

"Ohmigod," I said. I'd been meaning to call a plumber since Craig left about a year ago. For as long as I could remember, if you didn't jiggle the handle just right, the toilet would keep running. The next time you'd walk into the bathroom, there'd be a shallow puddle working its way out toward the door. Craig was convinced he'd fixed it every time it happened. He replaced the handle. He replaced some round rubber ball thing and probably some other things, too. But it always happened again eventually.

Craig was already jogging toward the door. "Come on," he said. "This can't be good."

The water in the bathroom was ankle deep and rising. "Get some towels," Craig yelled as he started untying his shoes.

"They're in the bathroom," I said.

Craig gave me a look, as if the towels had only started being kept in the bathroom linen closet after he moved out. I didn't want to deal with all that water alone, so I let it go.

"I know," I said. "I'll get some dish towels."

Of course, when I got to the kitchen I remembered I only had two, and neither of them was all that absorbent. So I grabbed two plastic bowls to bail out the water.

I went into the bedroom fast. I kicked off my shoes, pulled off my socks, and switched out my black pants for a ratty old pair of gym shorts. I made it back to the bathroom in time to see Craig wading through the water in the direction of the toilet.

"Ahoy, Matey," I said.

One of the legs of Craig's jeans came unrolled and landed in the water with a plop. "Shit," he said.

"Hope not," I said. He made a face.

Craig jiggled the handle. The toilet stopped running, and the room was suddenly quiet. I handed Craig a bowl. I scooped up some water with my bowl and dumped it into the sink.

Craig scooped some water with his bowl. "You're going to have to call a plumber," he said.

"Ya think?" I said. "Sorry," I added.

"That's okay. We probably should have called one years ago."

We bailed in silence for a few moments. The water made a little lapping sound around our ankles.

"Hey," Craig said. "Remember that time we were in Punta Cana, and the sailboat sprang a leak?"

"And the bailing bucket had a huge crack in it?"

"And we kept waving to everyone onshore for help, and they kept smiling and waving back?"

"That was so funny," I said. "Well, not at the time, but after." I poured out a bowl full and bent to scoop another one. "I was thinking about the time Lizzie was taking her sailing lesson in Marshbury Harbor, and the boat tipped over. You jumped off the side of that pier so fast."

"I thought she was going to kill me. But I mean, how was I supposed to know it was part of the lesson?" He squatted down in the water. "Hey, do you really think she should try culinary arts? I mean, she's such a creative kid. Her mother —"

"That bitch," I said.

Craig actually smiled. "God," he said. "Who knew life could get so complicated."

After we bailed out as much water as we could, we opened the bathroom closet and used the towels to wipe up the rest. Then I put the sopping towels in the washer while Craig set up an old fan in the hallway outside the bathroom door.

"Thanks," I said when he came into the kitchen, holding his shoes in one hand.

"No problem," he said.

The legs of his jeans had both come unrolled. They'd soaked up the water like a wick, and they were wet all the way up to his knees. I looked at them, then nodded at the dryer. "Do you want to put those in there?"

"So I don't catch my death of cold?" Craig's mother always worried about everybody catching their death of cold, and it used to be one of our favorite lines after leaving her house.

We stared at each other. "Boyohboy," I said. "You really messed things up."

"We both did. You barely talked to me that whole last year."

"Yeah," I said. "I guess. I couldn't think of a thing to say. I just kept thinking, *Is this all there is?*"

Craig shook his head. "I couldn't stop thinking about how every day when I woke up I was older than the day before. I still hate that."

"Oh," I said. "Poor baby."

I don't know exactly how it happened, but suddenly our arms were around each other, and then we were kissing. It felt both wrong and right at the same time, which actually might have worked as kind of a definition of our entire marriage.

I heard the sound of one of his shoes hitting the ground behind me. He started yanking at my clothes. I started yanking at his. It was like a throwback to the frantic excitement of when we were first dating, but it was also kind of angry, maybe even a little bit competitive, too. Whatever it was, it was hot, and by the time I heard the sound of the other shoe dropping, we were already halfway to the bedroom.

19

Having sex with my ex-husband turned out to be a lot like eating a hot fudge sundae. I really, really wanted it. The anticipation leading up to it was so heavenly it was almost painful. The first bite or two even lived up to my expectations.

Then, just as quickly, I was so over it. But what do you do? You've already bought it. And here the similarity fades, since it's a lot easier to dump an uneaten hot fudge sundae in the trash than it is to kick your ex-husband out of bed prematurely.

So, basically, I did what every red-blooded woman in America, or anywhere else for that matter, would do. I hung in there long enough to have a seriously overdue orgasm, and then I faked the rest of it. I made the right sounds and motions, but it was all I could do not to turn Craig's thrusts into a counting game, some twisted version of "Ninety-Nine Bottles of Beer on the Wall."

I'd once had a boyfriend back in my college days who swore he could do astral projection. I thought I might be doing it now. My body was on my bed screwing my former husband, and the rest of me was floating somewhere up by the ceiling, looking down at us and thinking, "Uh-oh."

I'd forgotten what a big racket Craig made when he came, but at least he finally did. I resisted the urge to ricochet out of bed and head for the hills. I shut one eye and kissed him beneath his ear.

He ran a finger between my breasts and down to circle my navel. "That was great," he whispered. "How was it for you?"

I'd completely forgotten until just this second. I kicked the covers off. "Precious," I said. "Cannoli."

Craig smiled. "That's new," he said.

I jumped out of bed and started looking for my clothes. "Hey," Craig said. "You look great. Have you been working out?"

I found my T-shirt. It was almost dark out, so I decided to just throw it on without taking the time to hunt for my bra, which was probably hanging from a chandelier somewhere. A cell phone rang down by my feet, and I picked it up.

"Don't," Craig said.

"Hello," I said.

"Hello?" Sophia's voice said.

I tossed the phone at Craig. "It's your girlfriend," I said.

Cannoli had her nose pressed against the glass door of the salon. Her tail started wagging a mile a minute when she saw me.

I opened the door and scooped her up into a hug. "I can't believe I forgot about you," I said. When Myles was first born, Tulia left him at the pediatrician's office one day. She put him down on the floor in his baby seat to write a check, then grabbed Mack and Maggie by the hands and headed out to the car. When she got home, there was a message from the receptionist telling her to count her kids again. Everybody had laughed for weeks about what a flake she was, but I was horrified.

Now I knew how easily it could happen. For the first time I wondered if I really could offer this sweet little dog a better home than the Silly Siren bride could. I put on a jacket and grabbed Cannoli's new jeweled leash and hooked it onto her collar. "Come on," I said. "I think we could both use a walk."

I held the leash in one hand and fished in my jacket pocket for something to soothe my ravaged lips. I pulled out a tube of Estee

Lauder Hot Kiss. "Not really," I said out loud, but I smeared it on anyway.

We were way down the street when Craig drove up beside us. He rolled down the window of his stupid leased Lexus. His hair was wet, so he must have taken a quick shower and used a washcloth to dry himself, since all the towels were in the washer.

He gave me a worried look. "Any ideas?" he actually asked.

"Yeah," I said. Cannoli and I picked up our pace, and I gave my ex-husband the finger over my shoulder. I couldn't believe he was actually asking me for advice. I couldn't believe I'd slept with him.

Cannoli and I walked for a long time. I peeked into people's houses the way I always did when I was outside at night. Most of them were watching TV. Nobody looked all that happy. Somebody had a butterscotch leather couch I really wanted.

I wondered what would happen if I just knocked on the door and asked where they'd bought it. Maybe a guy would answer the door, a guy who'd just slept with his ex-wife even though she was dating his brother, and he wouldn't want to talk about it with just anyone. We'd start with the couch, and the conversation would move on from there. Before we knew it, we'd realize that sleeping with our ex-spouses was just the first of many fascinating things we had in common.

I stopped on the sidewalk outside the house, still checking out the couch, until a woman walked into the room. She looked like she was yelling something over her shoulder.

I picked up Cannoli and started walking again. I buried my nose in what was left of her fur. It was nice and soft, and I was glad I'd taken the time to use some L'Oreal Vive Smooth Intense Anti-Frizz Mask, even though Sean Ryan had balked at the extra five minutes.

Eventually, we turned and headed home. It wasn't until we rounded the corner that I saw the flock of wild turkeys in the salon parking lot. Flock might have been an exaggeration, but I've never actually known how many it takes to make a flock. There were four of them, and they were walking right by the door to my apartment, as if they'd just come out of the salon after getting their feathers ruffled or something.

We slowed down and gave them time to pass. Cannoli didn't seem particularly worried about them, and the turkeys didn't even glance our way. They just plodded along, taking their time, heading toward a little break in the brush on the edge of the parking lot.

Wild turkeys weren't an unusual sight around Marshbury, especially as the town got more and more built up, and they had fewer places to hide. But still, it seemed like seeing them on this particular night, at this particular juncture in my life, had to be a sign.

Did it mean my former husband was a turkey? Or that I'd better get my life together fast, because Thanksgiving was practically right around the corner? Or maybe wild turkey was code for Wild Turkey, and it meant that I needed a drink.

"Let's go with three," I said to Cannoli as soon as the last of the turkeys had disappeared into the thicket.

Of course, sadly, I didn't really have any Wild Turkey in my apartment. The best I could come up with were two long-forgotten bottles of Sam Adams Boston Lager at the back of my refrigerator, tucked behind a molding cantaloupe I'd bought back when I was feeling healthy. I opened a bottle with one of my kitchen drawer pulls, a trick I'd learned as a Girl Scout, since Craig seemed to have absconded with the bottle opener at some point. I freshened Cannoli's water bowl and put the towels in the dryer.

I held up my beer bottle. "Cheers," I said.

Cannoli drank daintily, but I guzzled. What the hell was I thinking, sleeping with Craig? Was I trying to get back at Sophia? I didn't really think so, but it wasn't exactly a secret that I was much better at denial than introspection, so it was hard to tell. I thought. Then I drank some more. Then I got up and grabbed the second bottle. Then I drank and thought some more.

If I hadn't almost kissed Sean Ryan, I didn't think I would have slept with Craig. This might not make sense to a well-adjusted person, but what well-adjusted person sleeps with her ex-husband when he's sleeping with her half sister? I was pretty sure it was true though. Somehow my wires and hormones got crossed, and I got turned on and forgot to get turned off again. So maybe it was essentially like out-sourcing for sex. Or maybe it just seemed less scary to sleep with Craig than to have to start all over again with a new person.

I turned off the fan in the hallway outside my bathroom, brushed my teeth, peed for about ten minutes, and remembered why I never drank beer. Forget the antioxidants, Sean Ryan needed to come up with a beer that didn't make you have to pee like a racehorse.

I grabbed a towel out of the dryer and jumped in the shower. I slathered DHC Purifying Charcoal Shower Gel all over me. They advertised it as being able to absorb thousands of times its own weight in tarnishing toxins and beauty-clogging impurities. I hoped they weren't exaggerating.

I went into the bedroom, changed the sheets, and carried them into the kitchen. I put the sheets that smelled like Craig in the washer with extra bleach. Then I went back to the living room to call Sean Ryan.

"Hi," his voice said. "You've reached me, but I'm either off hang gliding in Argentina, or I'm not answering the phone. So leave a message."

"Hi," I said. "This is Bella. I'm just calling to say I'm sorry. That was weird back there in the salon, wasn't it? That guy was my ex-husband, in case you were wondering. Anyway, call me. And nice tip, by the way. Only kidding. Don't worry, I'll give it back. Okay. Bye."

I hung up the phone. I rummaged around the apartment until I found the invitation for Andrew's wedding. Saturday at 5 p.m. at some church, followed by a reception at the Margaret Mitchell House. The invitation was gorgeous, with beautiful copper foil insets. I turned it over and saw that it was made by an Atlanta company called Jack and Gretel. Ah, to believe in fairy tales again.

I picked up the phone and called Sean Ryan again. I waited out his message. "Hi again," I said in a voice that sounded way too chirpy to my ears. "Just wanted to let you know that my nephew's wedding is at five. So, how about I take half the table, all right, the left side, and then we'll have plenty of time to get to the wedding. So, call me and let me know when your flight is and where you're staying and how you want to meet up and all that. Okay, well, bye again."

Cannoli hopped up on my lap. We stared at the phone for a lot longer than we should have. Finally, I called Lizzie. "Hey," she said. "What are you doing up so late?"

I looked at the clock on the fireplace. "It's nine," I said. "I'm not *that* old."

She laughed noncommittally. "Did you talk to my dad yet?"

"A little bit," I said. "He doesn't sound completely against the culinary arts idea, but don't quote me on that, whatever you do. Maybe you should just pursue it on the side for a while. I mean, can you start a cooking club or something?"

"I already signed up to work on a cooking

show for the campus TV station. I figure it'll give me something to put on my résumé."

"Great," I said. I got up and walked into the kitchen to get a bottle of water from the refrigerator. After sleep, water is our second best friend. Or maybe we have two best friends. Anyway, once you start to dehydrate, it's all downhill from there.

I leaned back against the kitchen counter and took a long sip. Lizzie was still talking a mile a minute. "And," she said, "they're going to let me cook and everything. I've got my Radiator Ramen Noodles recipe down to a science. If you run the hot water in the dorm bathroom long enough, you barely even need to put the noodles on the radiator. But I'm going to keep that step in because I really like the name."

She paused to take a quick breath, and I heard loud music playing in the background. She sounded great. "And," she continued, "I even figured out how to make grilled cheese sandwiches with a travel iron."

"Genius," I said.

"It works perfectly. Plus, every freshman brings a travel iron to school and, like, who ever does any ironing?"

"Hey," I said. "I haven't had the chance to tell you this yet, but I'm working on a beauty kit. An entrepreneur has been giving me advice about it. I even took it to a college fair."

"Oh, that's so cool. Can you send me one?"

"Sure," I said. "I'll put it right in the mail."

"Thanks. Hey, do you think maybe you could help me make a cooking kit? You know, it might make it easier for me to get a real show when I graduate?"

I weighed an image of Craig and his first former wife both screaming at me at once against a picture of Lizzie and me hanging out together and working on her kit.

"Sure," I said. "I'd love to."

"Cool," she said. "Listen, I have to go. We're getting ready to go out in a few minutes."

"Actually," I said, "I am, too."

20

After I hung up with Lizzie, I checked my voice mail to make sure I hadn't somehow missed a message from Sean Ryan. Then I called Mario.

"What are you doing up so late?" he asked.

"Hey, it's Saturday night. I was just getting ready to go out."

Mario laughed. "Okay, seriously. What's up?"

"When are you and Todd heading to Atlanta?"

"Wednesday. We want to spend some time with Andrew, and we've still got a few things to check on for the rehearsal dinner. Why? And when's your flight?"

I sighed. "I was just making conversation. And Friday afternoon."

"Well, whatever you do, don't you dare bring that dog with you."

Mario took a sip of something. I pictured him stretched out on the couch with Todd, both of them sipping a nice red wine, talking about how a week from today their son would be married. Their shoes kicked off, a fire probably crackling in the fireplace even in August. It was like a goddamn Norman Rockwell painting. I wondered if I'd ever have a shot at a normal life again.

I sighed again.

Mario sighed, too.

"Okay, you first," I said.

"I can't stop thinking about Julie. How much fun she'd have with a reception at the Margaret Mitchell House, and how we'd both be doing our Scarlett imitations every time we talked to each other. What her dress would look like. The way I'd do her hair. How much she'd like Amy. How happy she'd be to see Andrew this happy. How much it sucks that she didn't get to see this."

Julie was Andrew's birth mother. She and Mario had been best friends since high school, and until the day she died, our father held out hope that she'd manage to turn Mario straight. She spent a night with a guy when she was in graduate school and ended up pregnant. He never called her again, and she decided to have the baby alone. Mario was her labor coach. She put his name on the birth certificate. Mario met Todd, Julie got cancer when Andrew was four, and Mario and Todd agreed to raise Andrew if she didn't make it. She didn't make it.

My eyes teared up. "You really loved her, didn't you?"

"Yeah," Mario said softly.

"Are they going to mention her in the ceremony?"

"I wanted them to, but Andrew said no. He wants Todd and me to get full credit as parents. He hates it when people want to know who his *real* parents are. So we decided Todd and I will just mention her when we give the toast."

"He's such a good kid. And I think it's great that you're both his best men."

"Yeah, he really is. Julie would be so proud of him."

I let out a cross between a sigh and a sob.

"Bella? What's going on?"

"I slept with Craig."

"No. You didn't."

"Oh, yeah."

"A week before Andrew gets married? What were you thinking?"

"Gee," I said. "Talk about the whole world revolving around you. I didn't exactly take out my calendar and check for conflicts."

"Does Sophia know? She's going to be a mess."

"Sophia?" I said. "Sophia? Why is everything always about Sophia? Listen, just don't tell anyone except Todd, okay? I'm pretty sure it'll just blow over. And besides, I'm bringing a date. That's okay, isn't it?"

"Sure," he said. "As long as it's not Craig."

By morning I was completely over men again. I mean, who needed them. I was going to get control of my own life, set some goals, and start moving forward from there. I got up early and did some crunches.

I put on my latest lipstick, a great OPI red called My Chihuahua Bites. A lot of people don't realize that OPI makes lipstick to match their more famous nail polish. Yucatan If U Want, also from the OPI Mexican collection, was a good one, too. Usually I didn't let myself read the label before I saw the color. I mean, how could you walk away from a lipstick called Who Comes Up with These Names? Even if you don't look good in caramel. Fortunately, My Chihuahua Bites was a keeper.

I took Cannoli for a walk. I picked up the phone and called the airlines. I'd thought about sneaking Cannoli on in my shoulder bag, but I wasn't sure what would happen if we got caught. Luckily, the flight hadn't reached their two-animal per-plane quota, so I made a reservation for her. It was ridiculously expensive, in my opinion, especially since I had to count her as one of my two carry-ons, which didn't seem fair.

Then I dialed the hotel. "Hotel Indigo, the intelligent and intriguing choice," a friendly male voice said.

"Are you intelligent enough to be pet friendly?" I asked politely.

"Is the pope Catholic?"

"Did my father tell you to say that?"

"Who's your father?"

"Never mind." I gave him my reservation number and Cannoli's name.

"See y'all soon," he said. "And it will be our pleasure to host Cannoli at no additional charge."

I figured this balanced being gouged by the airlines. "Thanks so much, y'all," I said. It was nice to know there were still businesspeople with a conscience out there.

After I hung up, I ate a bowl of cereal, because breakfast is the most important meal for beauty, drank a cup of coffee, because I needed it, and took out my kits. I turned one over and over in my hands. I knew there was a basic flaw in my kit design, and I finally put my finger on it. The thing was, a kit needed to function without the kit maker having to be there. And mine only worked if I was around to match and mix the foundation, and fill out the product recommendations and makeup instructions. Therefore, my kit could only sell if I were physically there to sell it. And consequently, it would never sell in big numbers.

Whew, it was nice to finally isolate a problem I could do something about. But what? What did the guidance counselor's kit have that allowed it to function while the guidance counselor stayed at school and counseled? It taught kids to write their own essays, instead of writing them for them. Although, come to think of it, that slacker guidance counselor should at least offer to check the essays to make sure they were good. Those poor kids could be sending anything off to those colleges.

"Bingo," I said to Cannoli, who was curled up on the floor, napping in a stream of sunlight. Even though she was sleeping, her tail gave a little wag at the sound of my voice.

While Cannoli slept, I got busy. What if inside each kit there was a postage-paid envelope, plus a questionnaire, as well as instructions to enclose a close-up photo without makeup? Then I could mix the foundation and fill out the diagrams, and also include specific tips for product application and suggestions for products. Maybe I could reach out to some companies for product samples. Maybe I could even charge them for product placement.

Wait. Wait. Who needed snail mail? I could design a Web site, so we could do the whole thing online. Then I could submit listings to some search engines, get the word of mouth going through our salon customers, and even try to get on some of the Boston televisions shows for some extra publicity. I was a lot more charming than half the guests I'd made up for them.

I was so excited I almost pulled a Tom Cruise and started jumping up and down on the furniture. I completely got the whole entrepreneur thing now. The thrill of figuring out a new project was amazing. Maybe even better than sex. At least if you were talking about sex with your ex-husband.

I pushed that thought out of my mind fast. I found some paper and got busy.

Bella's Bag of Beauty Basics
The Questionnaire

1. Please upload a close-up color photo of you at your worst — no makeup, harsh outdoor lighting. No worries — only Bella and her hardworking team of talented

beauty professionals will see it.

2. Fill out the following:

Name _____

Age _____

Ancestry _____

Single or Coupled _____

3 words to describe your personality

_____

3 words to describe your wildest dreams

_____

Biggest makeup problem

_____

Best feature _____

3. Find a magnifying mirror and look into the whites of your eyes. Are the lines radiating out from the center yellow? (If so, you have yellow undertones and you are WARM and will use the WARM color chart.)

Are these lines gray? (If so, you have pink undertones and you are COOL and will use the COOL color chart.)

4. Click on the appropriate color chart link below (either WARM or COOL). A new page will open. Print the chart and cut into individual color squares.

In the mirror (preferably the exterior mirror of your car, for best natural light), hold each of the eight colors up to your chin line one at a time. Pick the one that is the closest match and select it onscreen. Beneath your selection, make additional comments that might be helpful, for example — *slightly lighter than this* or *close, but no cigar,* or even *my printer sucks, so I'm just guessing here.* Also feel free to include the brand and shade of the foundation you're currently using in the space provided for comments.

5. Eye Color Chart. Check the color that matches your eyes most closely. Again, use the space provided to add your comments.

6. Hair Color Chart. Select the color that matches your hair most closely. (Not your natural color, should you happen to remember it, but your CURRENT hair color. If you know the product name and shade, please include it in the comment area.)

7. Vibe. Choose the celebrity whose style reminds you most of your own. Diane Keaton, Britney Spears, Melissa Etheridge, Olympia Dukakis, Joy Behar, Madonna, Nancy Pelosi, Gloria Steinem,

Lindsay Lohan, Oprah Winfrey, Sheryl Crow, Beyoncé Knowles, Courtney Love, Heather Mills, Jennifer Lopez, Jennifer Aniston, Whitney Houston, Angelina Jolie, Diane Sawyer, Robin Roberts, Ann Curry, Meredith Vieira, Kirstie Alley, Hillary Clinton, Shakira.

8. Best Color. Select the one color you're most likely to be wearing when you get a compliment.

That's it! Just press Continue to fill out your address and credit card info, and Bella's Bag of Beauty Basics will be back at you with your individualized, customized, and personalized makeup plan. Your kit will be beautifully packaged and include customized foundation, a magic elixir (just add two drops if your foundation looks too pale next summer), plus product samples and a personalized diagram with individualized product suggestions for eyes, cheeks, and lips. *Bellisima!*

I'd found some great template-based Web design software when I designed our salon Web site, so I spent the afternoon downstairs at Salon de Paolo registering the domain and working on a site for Bella's

Bag of Beauty Basics. Then I took a break because I couldn't wait to put a kit together for Lizzie.

21

The salons were usually closed on Mondays, but since we were going to be closed on Friday and Saturday because of Andrew's wedding, my father had decided to make Monday Friday this week. "Rome wasn't made to be a day," he said whenever anybody complained that this might be too confusing, which, of course, was even more confusing.

Our weekly or "standing" appointments had been jammed into Thursday. Friday appointments for customers who came in less often and had flexible schedules had been moved up to Monday, but Tulia's mother, Didi, didn't want to give up her Monday morning kickboxing class. Since she was the Friday receptionist at Salon de Lucio, the rest of us were taking turns answering the phone until she showed up.

"Did you hear about Celeste Sullivan?" Esther Williams asked as I parted her hair and clipped half of it out of the way with a long metal duckbill clip. "Keeled right over in the middle of a bridge game. Two days short of her eighty-ninth birthday. That's why I couldn't wait till Thursday."

"Oh, that's awful," I said.

"Too young," Esther Williams said. "She'll get a great turnout at the wake tonight, but the funeral might be only fair to middling. There's a Senior Center trip to Foxwoods, and the tickets are nonrefundable. It's a tough call. She loved Foxwoods."

I'd decided to teach Cannoli, who was wearing her black and white KARMA'S A BITCH T-shirt today, to be my assistant. She was turning out to be highly trainable, maybe even gifted. Just since I'd started setting Esther Williams's hair, she'd already learned to fetch the plastic curlers that I dropped and hold them hostage until I gave her a doggie treat. I'd had human assistants who didn't show half the promise.

Mario walked by. "Don't let Dad catch you doing that," he said. "Hey, that's not the same dog, is it?"

I shook my head. It was a relief to know the disguise was working. Esther Williams was checking out Mario as he walked across the room. "By the way," I said to her, "this is my new dog, Cannoli."

Esther Williams put on her glasses and leaned over the side of the chair so she could see Cannoli. "Well, doesn't that look like a rabies shot waiting to happen. It better not be drooling on those curlers, Missy."

"Don't worry. She'd never do that." I took a closer look at Esther Williams. "Are you okay?"

Esther Williams put one hand on her chest. "I don't like going anywhere on a Monday. I read somewhere it's the most common day for a heart attack."

"Don't worry," I said. "I read somewhere it's the most common day for finding a husband, too."

"You don't say," she said. I gave her a minute to look around the room for potential husbands. Then I put the next pink curler in.

My father came walking by, carrying a grappa-size package under his arm and shuffling through the latest stack of letters from Realtors and developers.

"Nice to be wanted," Mario said.

"Don't think I don't know who's behind it," my father said. He held one hand against his neck, then extended his fingertips, kind of popping them off the end of his chin in the direction of The Best Little Hairhouse in Marshbury.

My father was wearing camouflage pants and a rib knit sweater that picked up on the army green. I grabbed a curler out of Cannoli's mouth before he saw it. "Hi, Dad," I said. "How's it going? Is everybody loving that shiny new head of yours?"

"Is the pope Catholic?" my father said. He noticed Esther Williams and picked up his pace.

"Is that you, Lucky Larry Shaughnessy?" Esther said. "Come over here so I can get a good look at you."

The phone rang. "Your turn, Bella," Angela yelled across the room from her station.

I scooped up Cannoli and jogged over to the phone. "Good morning, Salon de Paolo," I said. "I mean Lucio."

The voice on the other end said something that sounded like *cost of fog*. I knew that voice.

"Excuse me?" I said.

He said it again, but this time it sounded more like *lost of dog*.

My heart started to beat like crazy. "I'm sorry," I said. "I think you have the wrong number." And then I hung up.

The phone rang again. I walked away.

Mario picked it up. "Salon de Lucio," he said. "What? That's ridiculous. We've never

230

had a problem with it. Okay. Okay."

"Dad?" he said after he hung up. "That was somebody from the town. They said they got a complaint that our septic system is failing. They're sending somebody over to test it. You know these old systems never pass inspection."

It would be hard to find anyone in Marshbury who hadn't heard a septic system horror story. Title V, which detailed the state's stringent septic regulations, was meant to protect the environment from faulty systems, but there were lots of people in town, particularly elderly people, who could barely afford to pay their skyrocketing property taxes. If a septic system failed, or worse, if someone anonymously reported it failed to the health inspector because they wanted to get their hands on the house, a person might be forced to sell their home if they couldn't afford to put in a new, expensive septic system.

And even if they could afford it, a septic system for a waterfront property, like the one my father's house and Salon de Lucio sat on, might have to be raised up out of the ground, so it wouldn't contaminate the harbor. Nothing like walking out the door to a big hump of grass-covered septic system between you and your view.

My father crossed his arms over his chest. "It's that hairhouse, I know it is. They've got another thing coming if they think they're going to put me out of business."

"Are you sure she doesn't look like a Chihuahua/terrier with a dye job?" I asked Mario.

"Honestly, it looks completely different," Mario said.

"Cannoli," I said. "Call her Cannoli. Come on, practice saying it, everybody."

"Cannoli," everybody said in unison. We were all sitting around waiting for my father to show up for the Friday meeting, which had been switched to Monday along with the rest of the day.

Ever since the *lost of dog* call, I'd known it was just a matter of time before the Silly Siren father of the bride showed up. By now I was such a wreck I was practically starting to twitch. "Tell me what you think she looks like," I said.

Vicky stopped dusting. "A dog," she said. Her Road to Responsibility coach looked up from her magazine.

"Thanks, Vicky," I said. "I don't know, I think she looks more poodle than terrier now, but I can still see some Chihuahua. Maybe we can pass her off as a chawoodle."

"Or a poowawa," one of the stylists said. She and another stylist were straightening each other's hair with a flat iron today. I was kind of wishing I'd thought of doing that with Cannoli's fur, instead of buzzing it off. Maybe I could have turned her into a mini-Afghan.

"Okay," I said, as soon as I gave my lips a calming hit of Maybelline Peach Colada. "The important thing is that we all get the story straight. Cannoli came from a breeder in Italy, and she's been with us ever since the salon opened."

"Wouldn't that make her two hundred and thirty-eight in dog years?" Todd said.

"Stop being such an accountant," I said. "We can't lose sight of the fact that she's not safe with that awful bride. Just remember, even if this seems like a small thing to you now" — I looked over at Sophia, who was glaring at me — "it might well save a dog's life."

My father usually entered through the breezeway door, but the salon door opened, and he came tiptoeing in, still wearing his camouflage clothes. He tucked the big rubber mallet he was holding behind the reception desk.

"That'll fix 'em," he said. He started snapping his fingers. Nobody moved.

"Lucky," Tulia's mother, Didi, said. "Now what did you do?"

Mario got up to look out the window.

My father was wearing his cat-who-swallowed-the-canary look. He rubbed his hand back and forth across the top of his head like he was polishing it. "Go outside and look across the street," he said. "One at a time, so it won't seem obvious, in case anybody's watching."

"I'll go," Mario said.

My father started snapping his fingers again, and by the time Mario came back we'd all moved our chairs into a semicircle. Sophia and I made sure ours were at opposite ends.

Mario pulled the salon door closed behind him. He was wearing a button-down shirt in a shade of rust that matched his freckles exactly. "The Best Little Hairhouse in Marshbury is for sale?" he asked.

My father slapped his knee.

"Dad," I said. "You didn't."

He pretended to zip his lips. Everybody got up from their chairs and started heading to the windows.

"Come on, Dad," Mario said. "We don't need trouble. It's going to cost us enough money if we have to put in a new septic system."

"Lucky, where'd you get the sign?" Todd asked.

My father gave his head another rub. "Lots of houses on the market these days, Toddy. It wasn't even a challenge, except they sure hammer those signs in deep. They're not as easy to pull up as you might think."

Tulia turned away from the window. "I don't get it," she said.

"What's not to get, my little bambino?" my father said. "Two can play at this game. They'll never put us out of business if everybody thinks they're on their way out of town."

The rest of us were still looking out the window. "Ooh," one of the stylists said. "Here comes the hairhouse. This is so dramatical."

Mario looked out again. "Wow," he said. "Those two wouldn't slip under anybody's gaydar."

"I told you," my father said. "I'm doing my part, but the rest of you are going to have to start dressing a little bit flashier around here."

The salon door swung open. The two guys walked in. Both were wearing skin-tight jeans and T-shirts that were even tighter. They had blond-streaked hair, perfectly arched brows, and I thought perhaps I detected a hint of Botox. I squinted to see if their faces moved when they talked.

My father put his hands on his hips. "I'm sorry," he said. "But we don't take walk-ins."

"Like we'd even consider it," the taller and blonder of the two said.

"Good thing," my father said. "Because I'm a beautician, not a magician." He bent over and slapped his knee.

The tall guy ignored him and held up a FOR SALE sign. "Know anything about this?"

My father laced his fingers together on top of his scalp. "About what?"

I felt like I was in an old western. I took a step forward. "Listen," I said, "there's plenty of room in this hair town for all of us."

"Tell that to the old man," the tall one said.

The shorter guy spoke up. "You know, you're not the first homophobe we've met in our lives, Gramps."

"Hey, watch that big *bocca* of yours, sonny boy. I even have a gay of my own. Two if you count the husband."

Mario and Todd waved. "He's not very PC, but he grows on you," Todd said.

"Say you're sorry about the sign, Dad,"

Mario said. "And promise you won't do it again."

"*Sei pazzo!*" my father yelled. "That means 'you're crazy,' for the non-Italians in the room," he added.

"Which would essentially be everybody," I said.

My father started shaking his fist. "What kind of hairdresser drops a dime on his neighbor's septic system? *Scemo! Stupido! Cretino!*" He spit on the floor of the salon. "*Disgrazio!*"

Vicky walked over and started sweeping up the spit on the floor.

The Best Little Hairhouse guys shook their heads. "We have no idea what he's talking about," the shorter one said.

My father took a step forward. He made the finger-popping-from-his-chin gesture again. "*Disgusto!*" he yelled. Mario grabbed him by the belt loop of his camouflage pants.

The taller guy handed the FOR SALE sign to Todd. "Just keep him away from our salon, okay?"

As soon as they left, Cannoli ran over to the door and started barking.

"A little late, don't you think?" I said.

"That's not a dog in my salon, is it?" my father asked.

"Okay, let's not get testy, everybody," Mario said. "We've got a big week ahead of us."

"So, is Andrew all set for the wedding?" Angela asked when we all sat down again, except for my father, who'd gone back to the house to get a bottle of grappa. "By the way, we're not leaving until Saturday morning. The kids have Friday afternoon soccer games they can't miss."

Mario smiled. "I think he's getting a little bit nervous about the wedding. He hates being the center of attention."

"Mike wanted to work late on Friday and meet the kids and me there on Saturday," Tulia said. "I said no way, so we're all flying down together Friday afternoon. Maggie still can't believe she really gets to be a flower girl at her cousin's wedding. And Andrew was so nice to ask both Mack and Myles to be ring bearers. I just hope Myles doesn't eat the ring. He's in an oral phase." The kids weren't with her today, unless she'd forgotten to take them out of the car.

"Well, they're the perfect age," Angela said. "My kids loved it when they were in Bella's wedding."

"Let's not go there," I said.

"You know," one of the stylists said, "I keep thinking it's Friday night, and it's almost time to go out." She shook her head. "It's very disorganizing."

There was a knock on the door. "I wonder who that is," Sophia said. She looked at me and smiled. It wasn't a nice smile. She got up and started walking to the door.

The door opened. It was the Silly Siren father. I grabbed Mario's arm.

"Hi," Sophia said. "Looking for something? Maybe with four legs?"

Mario peeled off my hand and stood up, too. "Nice to see you again, sir," he said. "Can I help you?"

I hunched over Cannoli so she wouldn't be so noticeable. Mario walked past Sophia and told the Silly Siren father we were in a meeting. He opened the door, and they walked outside together. Sophia paused at the doorway. The rest of us all leaned forward in our chairs, trying to hear them.

Sophia turned around and looked right at me. "I can't believe you're trying to take his daughter's dog away from her," she said.

"Look who's talking," I said. "Care to discuss who took what from who?"

Vicky looked up from sweeping. "Whom," she said.

"Wow," one of the stylists said. "She has good grammar."

"Not good," another stylist said. "Well."

Sophia and I were still glaring at each other when Mario came back in, holding the pizza.

"What happened?" about half the people in the room all asked at once.

Mario put the pizza boxes on the reception desk. "Okay, here's the official story. I told him you brought the dog back here because you didn't know what else to do. And when no one came to get it, I had to drop it off at the Marshbury Animal Shelter because we already had a salon dog. One who was known to be vicious with other animals. Killer Cannoli."

I got up and gave Mario a big kiss on the cheek. "You're the best," I said. I held up Cannoli so she could give him a kiss, too. "Did you hear that, Killer?"

My father came back with the grappa and opened a pizza box. He held up a slice. *"Mangiamo!"*

We started reaching for the paper plates. "Did we have the meeting yet?" one of the stylists asked.

22

It was great to have a focus. I'd been working almost round the clock and had a pile of kits all made up with nowhere to go. Once I finished the design and uploaded my Web site, I'd be in business. Lizzie's kit was already in the mail. I'd been buying her makeup since she'd first asked for lipstick just like mine, so I knew exactly what would and wouldn't work on her.

I mixed up her foundation first. She had tawny hair, deep brown eyes, and cool medium skin, so to make her eyes pop, I also added some Revlon Molten Metal eye shadow in a gray-blue called Scene Stealer and a Bobbi Brown long-wear gel eyeliner in Sapphire Shimmer Ink to her kit. I didn't put in any more makeup, because I wanted an excuse to send her another package soon.

At the last minute, I'd decided to throw in four coupons for free online makeup kits for Lizzie to give to her college friends. I mean, why couldn't I do a little bit of buzzing of my own? Plus, they could be my guinea pigs to make sure all the questionnaire links worked on my Web site. And their feedback would be a big help in fine-tuning the process. My goal was to make sure my foundation and product suggestions were as accurate online as they were in person.

I put the rest of the kits in a box on one of the closet shelves Craig had abandoned. My latest idea was that if I filled up all the space he'd left, I could make him disappear for good. I'd called the plumber, too, and now that the toilet was fixed, I couldn't imagine needing my ex-husband for anything ever again.

It was somehow Thursday night already. I couldn't believe Sean Ryan hadn't called me back yet. I mean, after all, sharing his table in Atlanta had been his idea. Even that almost kiss was his idea in the first place, if I remembered correctly. And I'd called him not once, but twice, so in the age-old game of telephone tag, he was clearly, indisputably It.

All week long I'd been sure Sean Ryan was going to call me any second. I even made up excuses for why he hadn't called yet. Emergency excuses, like sick relatives.

Entrepreneurial excuses, like antioxidant issues at the microbrewery. Even psychological excuses, like he was afraid of falling for me.

I not only made up several excuses under each category, but I'd also played our entire telephone conversation in my head. I'd accepted his apology and forgiven him completely. We'd made our plans for the college fair and the wedding. And still not a word from him. I hated that.

I started packing my suitcase for Andrew's wedding. I'd bought a great dress this week, while I was waiting for the phone to ring. It was a silk crepe halter with a deep V-neck, a ruched bodice, and a soft fluid knee-length skirt. The vibrant blue worked well with my dark hair, pale skin, and green eyes, and it also saved me from having to buy a new outfit for Cannoli. It matched the bridesmaid dress she'd been wearing when I'd met her perfectly.

Cannoli watched me put her cornflower blue taffeta bubble dress in the suitcase. "Don't get any ideas," I said. "You're definitely not going to the ceremony, and I'm not even sure I'll be able to sneak you into the reception."

She jumped up on the bed and put her front paws on the edge of the suitcase. "Oh, don't be so dramatic," I said. "Of course, you're coming with me. You just might have to spend a few hours hanging out in the hotel room by yourself, that's all."

After I packed a weekend's worth of clothes for both of us, plus dog food and toys, I pulled the box of kits back down from the closet. I decided I'd fill the rest of the available suitcase space with as many kits as I could fit. As long as I was buzzing them to college kids, I figured I might as well hand some out around the hotel during the downtime before and after the wedding.

I wasn't sure whether I should mix the foundation and write a list of product suggestions for people, or if I should just give them a coupon to get them to my Web site. In the end I decided it would be more impressive to give them an actual kit. My family still didn't know about the kits, which might complicate things, but I could be discreet when I concentrated. And, I mean, why shouldn't I do some test marketing in Atlanta, too?

I fed Cannoli at home, but I wanted to wait and pick up a salad at Marshbury Marketplace for me. I'd eat it on the beach while I let her run around. Even though it was still August, you could really feel fall in the air the last few days. I knew it would get hot again, but it was still a reminder that summer didn't last forever. Plus, I wanted Cannoli to be good and tired before she had her first plane ride tomorrow. At least the first plane ride that I knew of.

I wondered what had happened when the Silly Siren father went to the Marshbury Animal Shelter. Maybe I'd get lucky and it would turn out he just picked out another dog and hoped his daughter wouldn't notice. Since he hadn't come back to the salon again, it might mean the crisis was over, and we could all live happily ever after now.

Or possibly the fact that the Silly Siren bride hadn't shown up at the salon with him meant she wasn't all that interested in getting her former dog back, that she'd just asked her father to stop by and look for her if he happened to be in the neighborhood. Maybe the Silly Siren father hadn't even bothered going to the shelter.

It was starting to get dark already, so Cannoli and I had the beach pretty much to ourselves. She ran right down to the edge of the water and started rolling around on her back in a pile of seaweed and who knew what else. I decided to just let her go, since I was planning to give her a bath later anyway.

I flipped off the top of my salad and took out my plastic fork, which made me think of Sean Ryan again. Last time I'd been to this beach, we'd been eating fish and chips together.

I popped a cucumber slice into my mouth. Then I practiced chewing and being self-sufficient at the same time.

I still had Sean Ryan's business card in my wallet, and I took it out before I started up my car. His address wasn't exactly on our way home, but it wasn't really out of the way either. Plus, it was a nice night, and I liked to drive. And it was dark, so it wasn't like he'd see me if he happened to be looking out the window at the same time we were driving by.

"Oh, this is so high school," I said to Cannoli. "But I'm afraid we're going to do it anyway."

Cannoli stood up on her hind legs on the passenger's seat, but she was still too short to see out the window. "I'm sorry," I said. "I promise I'll get you some pillows. Or even a phone book. My grandmother on my mother's side used to have to sit on three of them just to see over the steering wheel. Did I ever tell you that? I guess we all got our height from our father's side of the family."

Cannoli looked over with interest. We pulled out of the beach parking lot and took a right. I flipped off the blinker when it didn't turn off on its own.

"I know," I said. "I'll be Thelma and you can be Louise. No, wait. You can be Thelma and I'll be Louise, because I'm more the strong, independent type. Okay, so, here we are, taking off for some girlfriend time, a simple weekend free of men. . . ."

Sean Ryan's house was in North Marshbury, and the beach roads we were taking to get there twisted and turned all over the place to hug the coastline, which added to the sense of adventure, in my opinion. I pulled over to the side of the road so we could put the top down. I just wished I had a scarf in the glove compartment to make me look more like Susan Sarandon in the movie. And too bad I didn't have a little matching doggy scarf for Cannoli. I mean, how cute would that be.

"We're just going to have to pretend we have scarves," I said out loud. "It's too late to go shopping, and we've got a busy day tomorrow." Cannoli didn't seem to have any problem with this. I lifted my shoulder bag from the floor to the seat, so she had something to stand on.

We found Sean Ryan's house right away, even in the dark, because it had a mailbox out by the road with big numbers on it. I'd been admiring this house for years. A little old man used to live there. Maybe he'd died or maybe he couldn't afford to keep it anymore. The house was white with black shutters and oozing with charm, originally part of a summer estate built back at the turn of the last century, probably a former maid's quarters. There was no way a maid could afford to buy it now. It sat up on a knoll and looked out over the cliffs to the open ocean. Sean Ryan must be one hell of an entrepreneur. Either that or a drug dealer.

His Prius wasn't in his driveway, but it could easily be in the detached garage. The outside light wasn't shining either, but I could see interior light peeking around the edges of the closed blinds in the downstairs windows.

I drove to the end of the street and made a U-turn. We cruised by again, more slowly this time. The interior lights were definitely on, which meant he was home. All my carefully thought-out excuses withered away. It certainly didn't look like he was in the middle of an antioxidant crisis. I leaned out in the direction of his house to see if I could hear his television blaring, but I couldn't hear a thing.

I turned down a side street, then pulled over to the side of the road, next to a wooded area between two houses. I put the car into park. Maybe I'd invent a new shade of lipstick called Thelma & Louise someday, but for now I had to settle for rummaging through my makeup kit until I found a tube of Chanel Crazed. It was a rich, dark shade, almost a pure brown, so it was practically camouflage.

My phone rang, and I jumped.

"Hello," I said, once I finally found my phone in my bag, which was under Cannoli.

"Hey," Craig's voice said in a whisper.

"Why are you whispering?" I asked.

"I can only talk for a minute. Listen, I'm probably not going to be able to talk to you at the wedding."

"What?"

"I mean, we've planned this for a long time, and she has her heart set on going. But, it's really not working out between us. I'm going to move into my Boston condo at the end of the month. The tenant's lease is up then. So."

Cannoli jumped over onto my lap. I ran

my hand along what was left of her fur. "Does Sophia know?" I asked.

Craig sighed. "Not yet. I don't want to ruin the weekend for her. But I wanted you to know. I've been thinking a lot about the other night."

"Craig?"

"Yeah?"

I probably shouldn't have dropped the *f*-bomb on my former husband quite so loudly in a residential area with my top down, but I did. Then I hung up on him and left him alone to revel in his own jerk-dom.

I put the car into drive. "Men," I said out loud. "They totally, totally suck. Who even needs them. Come on, Thelma, let's go. Just remember, sometimes you gotta kick butt and take names."

There was just enough light in the car for me to see Cannoli tilt her head and give me a quizzical look.

"I'm not really sure what that means either," I said. "But I like the way it sounds."

We drove faster on the way home. I was feeling a little bit footloose and fancy free. I wasn't quite ready to fly off the side of a cliff or anything, but I was definitely ready to shrug off the old and move on to something better.

I grabbed my kitchen phone before I could lose my nerve. Sean Ryan's machine picked up. Not only wasn't he calling me back, but he was probably sitting there screening his calls. Maybe he wasn't right up there on the jerkometer with Craig, but he was still a jerk. And so what if he lived in a nice house. I could make my own money. I could buy my own house. Maybe not that house, but so what.

"This is Bella," I said after the beep. "Listen, I'm just calling to tell you not to call me, okay? I mean, I've made a lot of mistakes in my life, but I really hadn't made any with you yet, so I think it's inexcusable for you to be this rude to me. And you should never have left me hanging like that about Atlanta and the left side of the table, not to mention my nephew's wedding. That's really bad form, especially for an entrepreneur, because you, of all people, should know better than to burn bridges, and let me tell you, this bridge is —"

A loud beep went off in my ear.

I looked at the phone. Then I called Sean Ryan's number again. "Anyway," I said, after I waited out his message and another beep, "in summation, I just want to say that we had our one moment in time, when the chemistry was there and our stars were aligned, and, well, you blew it. Okay, my ex-husband showed up and then I should have introduced you, so maybe those were factors, but you're the one who didn't call, which could have been a second moment, or even an extension of the first moment. . . ."

I heard another beep. I hated to end on a critical note, so I called one more time. "Sorry to take up so much space on your voice mail," I said. "But I just wanted to genuinely wish you a nice life. And, listen, when you get your hair cut the next time, make sure you go to a reputable stylist, especially since you can obviously afford one, and that whoever it is knows how to give a good razor cut. And, not to hurt your feelings, but you really were well on your way to a unibrow, so you've got to be careful about that."

I took a deep breath. "Okay, that's it," I said. "Good-bye, Sean Ryan."

After that, I slept like a log.

23

Cannoli and I decided to drive to Logan Airport and park there, since I wasn't sure whether either the Harbor Express water shuttle or the Logan Express shuttle bus were dog friendly. Hindsight twenty-twenty, I should have planned to carpool with one or more members of my family. I mean, after all, we were in the midst of a global warming crisis, and together we could have spared the environment some fossil fuel emissions.

Fortunately, it was midday, so the traffic on Route 3 wasn't too much of a nightmare. The airport tunnel hadn't dropped a roof tile and killed anyone lately, so I was pretty comfortable driving through it, though I did have a slight tendency to duck as I drove, I noticed.

We managed to find a space in Central Parking, so at least we didn't have to take a bus from one of the satellite lots. I pulled my suitcase out of the backseat of my bug, along with Cannoli's new travel case, a spiffy animal print pet backpack on wheels. When I first saw it, I thought maybe the dog was supposed to wear the backpack, but it turned out the person wore the backpack with the dog in it. It had a pull-up handle and wheels, just like my suitcase, so you could also roll it along on the ground. It had mesh vents in the front and on the sides to let in lots of air. I unzipped the top and popped Cannoli inside, then attached the safety harness to her jeweled collar.

She looked up at me in horror. "Don't worry," I said. "I won't zip up the mesh part until we absolutely have to."

I locked my car and made a note about where we were parked on my parking ticket, since I knew I'd never remember we were on the Swan Boats floor unless I wrote it down. Sunday night I'd be thinking, okay, now, was it the Boston Marathon floor or the Hatch Shell floor? Oh, no, maybe it was the Swan Boats floor. I mean, who thought up these names? There was a time and a place for creativity, and it sure wasn't the Logan Airport parking garage, if you asked me.

I extended the handles on my rolling suitcase and pet carrier, got them positioned evenly behind me, then hooked my shoulder bag over my head and under one arm, like a beauty pageant sash, so it wouldn't fall off. I reached back with both hands and started pulling. We moved along at a brisk, comfortable pace. The rolling suitcase was one of the best inventions ever, maybe right up there with the ionic hair dryer. I sure would like to have been the entrepreneur who thought up one of those two.

I heard a choking sound behind me. When I looked back, Cannoli was hanging from the backpack harness with her hind legs circling frantically in the air. She looked like she was riding a bike just above ground level.

"Cannoli," I yelled. I unhooked her and made sure she was breathing on her own. When I tried to get her back in the backpack, she whimpered. I talked to her soothingly yet firmly, then tried again. This time she started howling like I was hurting her.

People turned and stared as they walked by. "What are *you* looking at?" I said to one couple. I suddenly felt true remorse for every time I'd stared at a parent with a toddler throwing a tantrum. I made a vow to be a better aunt to Tulia's kids if I ever made it out of this parking garage. I pleaded with Cannoli one more time.

Finally, I just picked her up and put her in my shoulder bag. She poked her head out and calmed down right away.

I reached back and started pulling my suitcase and the empty backpack. "Don't think this means you won," I said.

I zipped Cannoli into the backpack just long enough to pay for her and check my suitcase, then as soon as we were out of sight, I took her out again. Fortunately, anything alive has to be carried through the walk-through metal detector, so that part was easy. One of the security women was a dog lover and even held her while I put my shoes back on. The world would be a better place if everyone just helped one another out when they needed it, in my opinion.

Practically the first person I saw when we got to the gate was my mother. She was dressed for traveling in pink sneakers and a bright turquoise sweat suit, and she was wearing one of her trademark red lipsticks, Cha Cha Cha by Estee Lauder.

I was happy to notice a subtle change in her hair color. Maybe she'd finally started using the Gray Chic by L'Oreal I'd suggested to her at least three years ago. My mother was one of those women who wear their gray hair like a badge of accomplishment. I say, okay, make your point, but at least get the yellow out with a shampoo like Artec White Violet, and brighten it up with a translucent finish like L'Oreal's Sheer Crystal.

We sandwiched my shoulder bag between us as we gave each other a kiss.

"I'm really sorry," I said. "I should have called you to see what flight you were on. We could have driven in together."

My mother glanced briefly over her shoulder. She turned back to me and shrugged. "We're all busy," she said.

I knew which buttons to push with my mother. "It's just that I've been trying to embrace my aloneness," I said. Cannoli popped her head out of my shoulder bag.

"I see," my mother said.

"I don't want to be one of those single women who put their lives on hold waiting to meet a man. Rather than learning to stretch and grow on my own."

My mother smiled. In the crowd behind her I caught a glimpse of a familiar shiny head. "Uh-oh," I said. "Don't look now, but I think Dad's on the same flight."

"Ciao, Bella," my father said a minute later. He reached an arm around my mother and handed her one of the two ice cream cones he was holding. They were both vanilla soft serve with chocolate sprinkles, which everyone around Boston called jimmies for some reason.

"Sweets for the sweet," my father said.

It almost sounded like my mother giggled, but the terminal was so noisy that it was probably just my ears playing tricks. "Yum," I said, looking at the cone my father was still holding. "That looks good."

My father kept his eyes on my mother. "About three gates down on the left," he said.

"Why, Lawrence Michael Shaughnessy," my mother said. "You remembered the jimmies."

"Why, Mary Margaret O'Neill," my father said. "It's not quite the gelato we had in Tuscany. Though I'd bet my favorite Dean Martin album we can find some of that once we get to Atlanta."

"Dean Martin was Italian?" I asked.

"Born Dino Crocetti," my mother said. My father beamed at her.

"All the great romantics are Italian," my father said. My mother beamed at him.

All this beaming was really getting on my nerves. My father was wearing an orange track suit with royal blue racing stripes. His red *cornicello* with the gold cap and thick gold chain really popped against it, and his black sneakers with the fluorescent green stripes added to the color burst.

"Wow," I said. "Guess we won't lose you two."

My parents kept licking their icc cream cones and looking at each other.

I squinted at them. "You two didn't actually drive in together, did you?"

"That's why they call it a personal life, honey," my mother said.

"That's not a dog in that backpack, is it?" my father asked.

"Okay, then," I said. "I guess I'll go find someplace to sit down."

"Fine, dear," they both said at pretty much the same time.

As soon as I found a seat out of earshot, I let Cannoli out so she could sit on my lap and called Mario's cell phone.

He answered on the second ring. "Don't tell me you missed your flight," he said.

"Oh, ye of no faith," I said. "I'm even early. How 'bout that?"

"Did you bring that dog?"

"Don't be ridiculous," I said. "Guess what? You're never going to believe this. Mom and Dad are on the same flight."

"Well, buffer it as much as you can, because they're just going to have to deal."

"Oh, they're dealing all right," I said.

"Believe me. It almost seems like they're flirting with each other."

"Well, I'm glad they're at least being civil. Maybe Dad's the date Mom was talking about bringing."

"That's hilarious." I checked my watch. "So, how's it going down there?"

Mario laughed. "Oh, it's an adventure, all right. One of Amy's uncles dragged us along for an impromptu bachelor party last night. At a big Atlanta strip club."

"Gay or straight?" I asked.

"Ha," Mario said.

I tried to read his voice. "Are they treating you and Todd okay?"

"Oh, they're fine with gays down here. It's northerners they hate."

"Cut it out," I said.

"I'm not kidding. Lots of tasteful little confederate flags flying everywhere. Apparently they're still fighting the Civil War."

"Who knew," I said.

"Just wait. I hear they're fixin' to fix okra at the reception."

"No," I said. "Will we have to eat it, do you think?"

"Everybody down here calls Andrew *Bahstin.*"

"What do they call you and Todd?"

"Bahs-tin. Or girlfriend. Depends."

"Oh, boy," I said.

A voice blared over the loudspeaker. "At this time we will begin boarding Flight Six Seventy-five with service to Atlanta and continuing on to Paris. We invite our first-class passengers, and those passengers traveling with small children or requiring a few extra minutes, to board."

"Listen," I said. "I gotta go. They're starting to board."

I hung up my phone, turned it off, and tucked it into my shoulder bag.

"Okay, Cannoli," I said. "You're going into the backpack again, and you're just going to have to deal with it until I can find a way to sneak you out."

I hooked the harness to her collar and zipped her in. I looked up. A handful of people, mostly wearing business suits and carrying briefcases, were working their way past the person taking the first-class boarding passes.

One of them turned around and waved.

It was Sean Ryan.

24

If I could have walked to Atlanta, I would have. I would even have climbed right onto the plane they used for filming *Snakes on a Plane,* if it could have kept me off this one. I would have seriously preferred to face all that venom wiggling down from the overhead compartments than Sean Ryan any day.

If only I could think of a way to get to coach without passing through first class. Whose idea was it to put it up at the front of the plane anyway? I could see the plane through the terminal windows, so I could tell it was one of the gigantic ones. There would probably be not one, but two aisles. That meant I had a fifty-fifty chance of picking the aisle that didn't go by him.

"At this time we will begin boarding zone E," the voice on the loudspeaker said so suddenly I jumped. "Please remove your boarding pass from the folder and have it ready as you approach."

Cannoli and I surged forward and funneled into a line with the rest of our group. I handed my boarding pass to the attendant, who held it under the scanner and handed it back. Halfway down the covered ramp to the plane, Cannoli started to whimper like crazy. I rolled her backpack over to the side.

A woman with shoe polish hair stopped beside us. "You better not be seated next to me," she said. "I'm allergic to dogs."

"She's totally hypoallergenic," I said.

The woman shook her head and started walking again. I resisted the urge to tell her I was allergic to her hair color. I unzipped Cannoli and popped her into my shoulder bag. "Be cool," I said.

"Hey there," a pretty blond flight attendant said as I walked up the covered ramp to the plane.

"Hey there," I whispered. I was trying to peek into the first-class cabin so I could figure out which was the safest aisle.

She took my boarding pass out of my hand, looked at it, then pointed to the far aisle. "This way, sugar."

"Thanks, sugar," I whispered.

I held my head high. I'd said what I said and that was it. Life goes on. I kept my eyes focused on the back of the plane. I had places to go, things to do, a seat to find.

People were taking forever to get their stuff up in the overhead bins, so the progress was painfully slow. We'd all take a step, wait some more, take another step. The guy in front of me was a real shedder. Short wisps of hair and huge flakes of dandruff drifted down the back of his black sports coat. I wondered if he'd tried Paul Mitchell Tea Tree Shampoo. Adding B vitamins to his diet might help, too, especially vitamin B6. A healthy head starts from the inside.

Cannoli wiggled her way up until her front paws were braced on the edge of my shoulder bag.

"Easy," I whispered. "We're almost there."

Cannoli jumped.

A woman screamed. "What *was* that?" somebody said.

I looked down. Sean Ryan was holding Cannoli, who was deliriously licking his face.

The pretty blond flight attendant pushed her way past the line. "All animals must be confined to approved carriers for the duration of the flight, or you will be asked to deplane immediately," she said.

"Gee," I said. "What happened to sugar?"

The flaky guy cleared his throat and let out an exasperated sigh.

"Hello. I'd like to get there *today*," some-body behind me said. I could feel people glaring at me from all directions.

My left arm, the one that was attached to the approved carrier, was twisted behind me. I gave it a yank. Cannoli's backpack crashed into my hip and then bounced against Sean Ryan's oversize first-class seat.

He grabbed it out of my hand and tucked it under the roomy seat in front of him.

The flight attendant flashed him a daz-zling smile. "Oh, sir," she said. "I didn't re-alize the bitty critter was with you. Can you just do me a favor and tuck him back into his little case until we get off the ground, sugar? I'll see if I can find him a cookie in just another minute."

I couldn't avoid it anymore, so I looked at Sean Ryan. He smiled.

"Lady," somebody said behind me. "Let's *go.*"

I reached down and scratched Cannoli behind her ear. "Traitor," I whispered.

There wasn't a lot to do once I got to my seat, and there certainly wasn't much room to do it in. I was on the aisle, but the woman next to me already had her arm on my armrest, and there was no way she was giv-ing it up. I leaned into her and tried to edge out an inch or two. No go.

So I closed my eyes and tried to pretend it was all a bad dream. Maybe Sean Ryan hadn't even checked his messages. Maybe he only used his cell phone and his home phone didn't even work anymore, and they'd just forgotten to disconnect the voice mail. Not that I'd done anything wrong. So, okay, I'd left a few messages. Where was the crime in trying to get a little closure? And it's not like I'd left that many of them. If the beep interrupts you, you don't have to count the next call as a whole separate message. Everybody knows that. And, bottom line, he was the one who should be embarrassed. What kind of guy tells a girl he'll go to a wedding and then disappears on her?

I opened my eyes and looked around. The glow of my father's scalp up ahead in coach caught my eye. He was tilted way over toward the seat next to him, where I could see a shock of gray hair. That was some great big coincidence that they'd ended up sitting together on the plane. I heard a burst of laughter that could only be my mother's.

I closed my eyes again.

"Bella," somebody whispered. I was in the middle of a dream. Craig was dressed like a plumber, with one of those big tool belts around his waist. His pants were hanging low, exposing an endless crack, and he was leaning over my toilet with a plunger.

"Sophia loves it when I wear this," he was just saying when I woke up.

"She snores just like you," Sean Ryan said. For a minute, I thought he was talking about Sophia. I wiped my hand across my mouth, in case I was drooling, and then rubbed my eyes, stalling for time.

Finally I looked up. Sean Ryan was holding Cannoli. It takes a lot of guts to walk around a plane with an uncrated dog, although he did have an airline blanket wrapped over his shoulders to conceal her.

"Is that what the other half wears in first class?" I asked.

He adjusted his blanket and raised a well-shaped eyebrow. "Do I sense some hostility directed at business travelers with a surplus of frequent flyer miles?"

While I was sleeping, the woman next to me had let her elbow drift from my half of the armrest to take over some of my personal seat space. I stretched and leaned into it, hard. "No, not at all," I said. "I'm happy for you and your miles. And once I can feel my toes again, I'm sure my disposition will improve."

"Do you want to switch seats for a while?"

he asked.

"That's okay," I said.

"I'll take it," the woman next to me said.

Sean Ryan and I looked at each other. I felt the same little jolt I'd felt back in the salon right before our almost kiss. He nodded his head toward the back of the plane.

"Save my seat," I said to the woman next to me.

A couple of flight attendants were standing in the back of the plane chatting, so we stopped in the aisle just in front of the two bathrooms.

A man walked up and stood behind us. Sean Ryan gestured to the bathroom. "It's all yours," he said.

"Thanks, pal," the man said.

"So," I said when he disappeared.

"So," Sean Ryan said.

We both waited.

"You never called me," I said.

He put a hand on my arm, then took it away. "Listen, I'm sorry. I was traveling this week, an island off the coast of Ecuador. . . ."

"Oh, puh-lease," I said. "Like they don't have phones in Ecuador."

He shrugged.

"And your lights were on. I mean, I bet your lights were on."

"They're on timers." He blew out a puff of air. Cannoli licked his cheek. "Listen, here's the thing. I have a business conflict. I didn't want to have to explain it."

"Ohmigod, so you are a drug dealer."

He shifted Cannoli in his arms. "What are you talking about?"

"What are *you* talking about?" I crossed my arms over my chest and looked right at him.

He looked right back at me. His hazel eyes had flecks of gold in them. "Okay," he said. "I should have called you. There really is a business conflict. I also have this bad habit of ending up as somebody's rebound relationship. No way I'm going there again."

At this point, I was so confused I couldn't quite remember whether I even wanted to go there anymore, or even where there was, for that matter. But the more he seemed to be rejecting me, the more I was convinced he might be wrong. I took a little step forward and tried to think of something brilliant to say. "But . . ." was all I could come up with.

"Listen," he said. "You hit the nail on the head. I think it was in your fourth message, although maybe it was the fifth." He smiled.

"Cute," I said.

"You were right about the stars. Timing *is*

everything."

I shut my eyes.

"I'm not denying the chemistry, Bella. You're smart, you're beautiful . . ."

I opened my eyes again. I was really starting to like this guy.

". . . and somebody is going to be lucky to have you in his life someday. But, I've been there. You've still got some stages to go through. You probably haven't even had hot sad sex with your ex yet."

My jaw dropped. The two people sitting on the aisle seats closest to us turned to look. I shut my mouth again. There was absolutely nothing I could say without incriminating myself.

Cannoli started trying to wiggle her way out of Sean Ryan's arms. He handed her over to me, then took the first-class blanket off and wrapped it around my shoulders.

"Fine," I said. "We'll just be kit buddies. Is the left side of your table still open tomorrow?"

Sean Ryan narrowed his eyes. "You brought your kits with you?"

"Never leave home without them," I said. He didn't say anything, so I decided to push my luck. "And you've got to eat, so you might as well come to my nephew's wedding."

Sean Ryan massaged his forehead with one hand. "Okay, you can come to the college fair," he said. "But, for the record, this goes completely against my better judgment."

"Relax," I said. "We'll keep a table length between us at all times."

"But not the wedding," Sean Ryan said. "I can't go to your nephew's wedding."

25

Sean Ryan had a business dinner that night, or at least he said he did. He offered to drop me off at my hotel, but I told him I had plans, which was a big fat lie.

After we got off the plane, he held Cannoli while I used the bathroom, then I watched his carry-on while he did. I looked around for an indoor patch of grass for Cannoli, who had the tiniest bladder of us all, but no such luck.

"Thanks," he said when he came out. I noticed he'd washed his face and tidied up his hair in the men's room. I wondered if he'd done it for me or for the person he was meeting for dinner.

"Don't do anything we wouldn't do," my mother's voice said behind me. She and my father giggled like a couple of kids and kept walking right by us.

"Do you know those people?" Sean Ryan asked. He grabbed his carry-on with one hand and Cannoli's empty backpack with the other.

I shook my head. "Apparently not," I said. "But they used to be my parents."

We watched them for a moment. Somehow my father's arm was around my mother's shoulders. Sean Ryan cleared his throat and looked away. "Well, isn't that nice to see," he said. "How long have they been married?"

"They're not," I said. "They hate each other. And I can't believe they're not worried about me. I mean, you could be anyone."

We started walking, my parents' sweat suits like faraway fluorescent beacons in front of us. We took an escalator down and stepped onto a tram. The Atlanta airport must have been about a million miles long. I kept thinking we were going to be in Texas by the time we got out, but it was only the baggage claim area.

"Okay, then," Sean Ryan said after we caught our luggage as it came by on the turnstile. "I'll pick you up tomorrow at your hotel at eleven."

"Don't be late," I said. I reached out my hand to shake his hand.

He laughed.

"Hey, you made the rules," I said.

He leaned over and gave me a little peck on my cheek, and I tried not to notice his Paul Mitchell Extra-Body Sculpting Foam. He reached over to pet Cannoli in my shoulder bag. "Take good care of her," he said. I wasn't sure which one of us he was talking to.

Sean Ryan, Cannoli, and I all followed the signs out to the ground transportation area. He turned right, so we went left. There wasn't even a hint of fall here. It was at least thirty degrees warmer than it had been back home in Marshbury.

There also wasn't one single bit of grass or dirt outside the airport. Even the median strip was a concrete sidewalk. Where did Atlanta's pet travelers pee? Maybe city dogs just learned to use the sidewalk. We kept walking. It looked like if we crossed the road that all the cars used to get onto the highway, we might come to a planted-up area, but we also might get killed.

Finally, I just lifted Cannoli up and plopped her down on a great big ashtray built into the top of a trash barrel. "Good thing you're not a German shepherd," I said.

She looked up at me in disbelief. There were a couple of cigarette butts and the nasty-looking remnants of a cigar, but as far as ashtrays went, it was pretty clean.

"Come on," I said. "Cats do it all the time. Just try to think of it as a litter box."

Finally her Chihuahua-size bladder won out. I glanced away to give her some privacy. Two women looked over and whispered something to each other, too polite to say it to my face. Clearly, we weren't in Boston anymore.

We walked back to ground transportation. I was pretty sure I remembered Mario telling me something about shuttles being available, but I wasn't sure if they would be pet friendly, so I decided to splurge and treat us to a cab.

"Welcome to Lannah," the cabdriver said.

"Who's Lannah?" I asked.

He laughed. "Where you headin', Ma'am?"

I put Cannoli down on the seat beside me and started rifling through my shoulder bag. "I think it's somewhere on Peachtree."

He looked at me in the mirror. His skin was the color of mochaccino, maybe a MAC NC30, with a sprinkle of freckles that looked like chocolate. "You gotta do bettah than that, Ma'am. They all Peachtree in Lannah."

I had no idea what he was saying, but I loved the melodic way it sounded. I found the address for Hotel Indigo and read it out loud to the cabdriver. We pulled out into the traffic.

I opened a water bottle and drank half, then fed some to Cannoli, since I figured she could handle it now. I looked out the window. I held Cannoli up so she could look out the window, too.

Most of the traffic was coming out of the city and toward us, but there was plenty going in our direction, too. The highway had so many lanes it made Boston look like the boondocks.

"Is the traffic always like this?" I asked.

"You should see it when the Chicken Pluckers Convention comes to town."

I laughed, in case it was a joke. He looked at me in the mirror. "Where you from, Ma'am?"

"Bahs-tin," I said, for the first time in my life. In a minute I'd be saying *Pahk the cah in the Hahvid yahd* on cue.

"Okay," he said. "I got one for ya. A couple from Bahs-tin was tourin' the back roads of Georgia. They'd seen the folk art and were fixin' to eat in an authentic Southern restaurant."

He put his blinker on and switched lanes. "They stopped at the first one they came to. The dinner menu consisted of grits, sweet tea, and chicken three ways. The Bahs-tin gentleman straightened his tie and said, 'Excuse me, Ms., but could you please tell us how you prepare your chickens?'

"The waitress took her time thinkin' about it. Finally she said, 'Well, sir, in these here parts we don't do anything real special. We just tell 'em straight out they gonna die.' "

"Did you get that one from the chicken pluckers?" I asked when I finished laughing.

"Drive 'em every year," he said. "We love 'em in Lannah. Those good ol' boys know how to eat, and they sure are fond of naked women."

That last part made me a little bit nervous, so I kept my mouth shut for the rest of the way to the hotel. Then, since I arrived safely, I gave the cabdriver an extra-big tip for the joke.

The hotel was on Peachtree Street, not to be confused with West Peachtree or Peachtree Road or Peachtree Place. Maybe I could leave a trail of peach pits behind us when I took Cannoli out for a walk, just to make sure we found our way back to the right Peachtree.

As soon as I saw it, I knew why Andrew and Amy had picked this hotel for everyone to stay in, even though it was closer to the Fox Theater than it was to the Margaret

Mitchell House. Hotel Indigo was the cutest boutique hotel ever, just the kind of place Mario and Todd would have picked. It was a funky little oasis in the middle of midtown, with a totally hip and welcoming indigo blue awning with a seashell on it over the entrance, and a front patio dotted with bistro tables and flanked by a flower garden. I didn't know where the chicken pluckers stayed when they were in town, but I was pretty sure it wasn't here.

In the lobby, we were greeted by another shock of indigo blue, with crisp white and soft green accents. "Oooh," I said to Cannoli. "Let's move here."

Cannoli was ignoring me. She strained at her leash, trying to reach a dog about her size, which was wagging its tail like crazy.

"That's Indie," the guy behind the desk said. "He's a Jack Russell terrier. Indie's the star of the show around here."

If I were an eight-pound Chihuahua/terrier mix with a dye job, I think I would have found Indie pretty hot, too. He was an inch or two taller than Cannoli, with a cinnamon face edged in nutmeg and a mostly white body. He had a strong, proud chest and intelligent eyes. I realized I was checking out a dog, which was more than slightly scary.

I finally dragged Cannoli away, after promising her that maybe Indie could go for a walk with us later. Our room was up on the third floor, facing Peachtree Street, and it was soft beige with an abstract mural on one wall, and black, white, purple, and green accents. The bed had a great white beadboard headboard that was beachy enough to make me feel at home. There was a cute haiku that made the tiny bathroom seem more poetic than inadequate, and the Aveda bath products were a nice touch, too. You can tell a lot about a hotel by its bath products.

We got our clothes hung up and everything else put away. I leaned back against the headboard and put my feet up on the bed. I flipped through the channels on the TV.

Cannoli walked over and sat right in front of the door. I ignored her. She started scratching at the floor. She let out a sharp bark.

"All right, all right," I said. "Wow, you've really got it bad."

Ten minutes later, I had my sneakers on, directions to Piedmont Park in one hand, and leashes attached to Cannoli and Indie in the other.

"Okay, you two, it says 'walk ten blocks

279

north on Peachtree Street, then walk about four or five more blocks down Tenth until you get to the park.' This better be worth it."

We worked up a good appetite getting there, so we stopped at a shacklike place called Woody's right across from the park. I got a delicious hot dog for me and one for the dogs to split. So far I was lovin' Lannah.

The dog park in Piedmont Park was easy to find — we just followed the dogs. There was a small-dog park within the dog park within the park park. It seemed like there should have been a song for it, maybe something like the old kids' song about the knee bone being connected to the shinbone.

Cannoli and Indie played like crazy, mostly with each other, but sometimes with Indie's other friends, whose owners all knew him by name. "Stayin' at the hotel?" a few of them asked me.

I nodded and smiled, and even told some of them about Andrew's wedding. Everybody was so friendly that at first I thought they were being sarcastic. They were well dressed in kind of an upscale, urban professional-looking way. I tried to imagine what it would be like to move to this warm, happy place where people talked to strangers. Maybe I'd find a place to live near Piedmont Park. Somewhere not over a hair salon. Somewhere nowhere near my family.

Then I pictured myself showing up at Andrew and Amy's apartment every Friday night with a pizza box, overcome by the urge to create a Marshbury South down here. Or, just my luck, it would turn out that my family was connected to me as if we were all wearing bungee cords. As soon as I'd move, then *boing,* Mario and Todd would spring here next, then Angela and her family, then Tulia and hers, then Sophia and my ex-husband. . . . Pretty soon we'd all be living on top of one another again. Maybe faux Italian Shaughnessys could only survive in a pack.

"Okay, you lovebirds, that's enough," I said finally, though I didn't really have anyplace else to go until 11 a.m. tomorrow.

We left the small-dog park, then the large-dog park, then found a bench in the park park. I poured some water from the bottle I'd bought at Woody's into a paper cup and let the dogs take turns drinking. They curled up next to each other on the ground. They looked so happy just lying there that I didn't have the heart to break them up.

I leaned back on the bench. From what I'd seen so far, all Atlanta needed to be perfect was an ocean. I wasn't sure if I could actually survive without the smell of salt air, the feel of sand between my toes when I walked the beach.

A few benches away from me there was a guy stretching. I couldn't see his face, but he was wearing shorts and sneakers and looked like he'd just finished his run. He had a nice long back, and his hamstrings looked pretty flexible, too. I kept looking away, then looking back at him. I was so drawn to him, as if I somehow knew him. Maybe he was the man I'd be with if I got up the nerve to move here. Maybe our stars were aligned, and strong chemistry was calling out to both of us.

Any minute he might turn around and say hi, or hey, as they said down here. I'd say hey, too, and he'd come over and ask me about the dogs. I'd tell him the whole story about Cannoli, and we'd just keep talking. And then he'd want to know if I'd had dinner yet.

The man finished stretching and turned around.

It was Craig.

26

"Geez, Louise," I said. "Can't I go any-where?"

Cannoli jumped to her feet and started barking away like a maniac. Indie joined her in perfect terrier harmony.

"What'd I do?" Craig asked as he approached. I wasn't sure if he was talking to me or the dogs.

"Where's your girlfriend?" I asked.

He shook his head. "Back in the room. We just got here this morning, and we're fighting already."

"Aww," I said. "Too bad."

Cannoli bared her teeth. Indie bared his teeth. Then they turned their backs and curled up on the grass again.

Craig nodded at the bench. "Can I sit down?"

"Knock yourself out," I said.

"You don't mean that literally, I hope."

"Ha," I said.

He sat down anyway. I slid sideways on the bench, away from him.

Craig leaned back against the wooden slats and crossed the legs I should have been able to recognize, even from the back, even in the South.

It was hard to remember what I'd ever seen in him. He'd come into the salon for a haircut one day about a dozen years ago, a referral from a co-worker of his who was a client of mine. I was attracted to him right away, in that way that you either are or you aren't. He was friendly and handsome, with sad eyes and fine, thinning hair.

Some clueless stylist had made a mess of his hair by texturizing it, something you should never do to fine hair. I gave him the illusion of volume with some stacked blunt layers. He smelled good. He was on his way to pick up his kids for the weekend. They were planning to go the aquarium. His ex-wife had the house in Marshbury; he'd bought a condo in Boston's South End. He seemed lonely. I knew I was. He asked me if I wanted to have a drink on Sunday when he dropped the kids back off at their mother's. I did.

"Did you call the plumber yet?" my former husband asked.

I had a brief flashback to my dream on

the plane. I pushed it away fast. "Yup," I said. "All fixed. So I guess I won't be needing you anymore."

"Can I ask you one thing?" he asked.

I shrugged.

"Why are you so mad? I mean, what exactly did I do wrong?"

"That's two," I said, even though I knew it was childish.

"Okay, pick one."

I took a sip of my water, then thought about whether I should offer it to Craig. On the one hand, I didn't want to get his germs. On the other hand, I'd had ten years to build up immunity.

I handed it to him. He took a sip and handed it back. We were both still staring straight ahead. "Thanks," he said.

"Listen," I said. "Neither of us did anything wrong. Everybody does it. It even has a name. It's called hot sad sex with your ex."

Craig covered his face with his hands. He arched his back and tilted his elbows up toward the sky. "And the sad part would be?"

I didn't say anything. Down in the grass, Cannoli and Indie both started to snore, their little bodies twitching in time to their dreams.

Finally Craig stretched his arms over his head. Then he put his hands on his thighs and stretched way out over his knees. "Hey," he said. "Lizzie called the other night. She's all excited about the cooking kit you said you'd help her make."

"It's not that big a deal. It'll probably turn out to be mostly recipe cards." I turned my head to look at him. "You're not mad?"

He turned to look at me. "No, not at all. You were always great with Lizzie. And Luke."

"What about Sophia?" I couldn't stop myself from asking.

Craig sighed. "She wants us to have kids of our own."

I looked down at my hands. They seemed to be peeling the label off my water bottle all on their own, as if they'd completely disconnected from my brain. "And, what, you'd rather lease a midlife Porsche?"

"It's just that I was hoping to have a few years off before I started gearing up to be a grandfather. Things were supposed to start getting easier." He ran his fingers back through his hair and looked at me with his sad eyes. "I can't stop thinking about all the things you and I were going to do once Lizzie went off to college."

I wished I'd thought to casually ask Sean

Ryan whether hot sad sex with your ex was a single or a multiple occurrence. Just in case, I was glad Craig and I were sitting on opposite sides of a park bench and it was still fairly broad daylight. I was pretty sure I didn't want to sleep with him again, but I hated the idea of never again waking up in the same bed with him. Or sitting around a table in a restaurant with Craig, Lizzie, and Luke, maybe celebrating Luke's graduation or first postcollege job, or Lizzie's first real cooking show.

It was an odd little sort of family we'd created on alternate weekends and holidays, but I'd loved being a part of it. And, sadly, there was no slicing it down the middle into an even smaller piece of the pie. Every third weekend and holiday didn't exist. Craig got it all, or what was left of it as the kids moved on to their own pies.

I stood up and threw the empty water bottle and the strips of label into a trash barrel. When I looked up, Craig was checking me out the way he used to a long time ago when he didn't think I was looking.

I'd tucked the ends of the dogs' leashes in between two slats of the bench, and I pulled them out now. The dogs both jumped up, ready to go. Cannoli bared her teeth and gave Craig a little growl.

"What did I ever do to her?" Craig asked.

"Word gets around," I said.

We walked back along Tenth together. I was kind of glad to have Craig with us, since it might up my chances of finding the right Peachtree and getting safely back to Hotel Indigo. A woman said, "Hey, how y'all doing today?" as she walked past us.

"Who was that?" Craig asked.

"No idea. I think she was just being friendly. Kind of scary, isn't it?"

"No shit," Craig said.

We both started to laugh. Then we really started to laugh, that great kind of out-of-control laughter that takes all your energy and starts to hurt after a while. We moved over to the edge of the sidewalk so people could get by us. The dogs tilted their heads and looked up at us.

"Oh, boy," I said.

Craig put his arm around me and kissed me on the forehead. "I miss you," he said.

"I bet you do," I said. "I'm totally missable. One of the most missable people I know, in fact."

"Yeah, you are," Craig said.

"Don't look now," I said. "But here comes Sophia."

I tried to remember if I'd ever stayed in a

hotel room by myself before. Or at least without human companionship, since Cannoli provided more than her share of the canine kind. I'd finally managed to pull her away from Indie in the lobby, after making plans for Cannoli to hang out with him at the hotel tomorrow while I went to the college fair and then to Andrew's wedding. Maybe I'd let her wear the bridesmaid dress anyway, just for Indie.

I felt bad about running into Sophia earlier. She'd turned around as soon as she saw us and started walking in the opposite direction. Fast. Craig ran after her.

Fortunately I wouldn't have to see them again until tomorrow. Andrew and Amy had decided to keep the rehearsal dinner small, just their parents and the people who were actually in the wedding. The sheer size of my family could be overwhelming. I guess the plan was to spring us on Amy's family gradually.

So I had the whole night off. It was a good opportunity for solitude, something I should learn to savor. I was kind of getting used to living alone now, though in the beginning it was tough. I'd never even had a bedroom to myself growing up. And I'd had roommates in college and after college. Then I lived with a boyfriend. Then I broke up with him, moved home, moved in with another room-mate, married Craig.

But now I was alone in a hotel room with nobody to answer to. I could keep the TV on or turn it off. I could kick off all the covers or leave them on. I could stay up till all hours reading a good book. Or go to sleep right now if I felt like it.

I called room service and ordered a grilled panini and a glass of sweet tea, just to see what it was like. I wolfed down the sandwich while Cannoli ate a can of dog food in a more ladylike manner. The sweet tea was another matter entirely.

"How can they drink this stuff?" I said to Cannoli as I dumped it down the sink in the bathroom. I brewed myself a cup of hot tea, no sugar, no nothing, in the coffee-maker.

I checked my dress for tomorrow. It was still pretty wrinkly, so I hung it up in the bathroom, along with Cannoli's, turned the shower on hot, and closed the door.

Ten minutes later, our dresses were wrinkle free. That left the rest of the night. I turned on the TV and flipped through the channels while Cannoli napped. Then I went back into the steamy bathroom and put some Hot Nights by Lancôme on my lips.

We moseyed on down to the lobby. There was no sign of Indie, so the two of us went for a walk down a Peachtree and back, two single women out and about in a new town, having a little girlfriend time, a simple evening free of men.

Since I hadn't taken the time to look in the mirror before we left, I used my favorite trick to keep any excess lipstick from landing on my teeth. You just pop your index finger into your mouth and pull it out. You might get a few looks, but any excess lipstick will come off on your finger. It was brilliant in its simplicity. I just wished there was a trick like that to tidy up the rest of my life.

We turned right and walked down another Peachtree. "I don't know about you, Thelma," I said, "but I'm bored to tears."

We went back up to our room. Cannoli lapped some water from her travel bowl, then took another nap. Maybe I should learn to nap. I packed up my kits for tomorrow. My cell phone rang. I ran across the room to get it.

"Hello," I said, without even bothering to look at the caller display.

"It's me," Mario said.

"Oh, hi. How'd the rehearsal dinner go?"

"You're not going to believe it. Throw some clothes on and come have a drink with

Todd and me. We're downstairs in the bar."

Cannoli was looking at me with her ears perked up. "Is there a cute little Jack Russell terrier down there?" I asked.

"Bella," Mario said slowly. "Don't you think you're starting to go a little bit over-board with this dog thing?"

"Don't worry," I said. "It wasn't for me. I was asking for a friend. I'll be right down."

Mario and Todd were sitting at the bar in high-backed indigo-painted barstools. "You guys look great in blue," I said.

"Thanks," they both said at once.

Todd moved over with his wine, and I climbed up on the stool between them. They both leaned over to give me a kiss. Cannoli came sauntering into the bar with Indie hot on her heels.

"Bella," Mario said. "Tell me that's not your dog. You said you weren't bringing it."

The bartender put a napkin in front of me. "Chardonnay, please," I said.

He poured three glasses of wine and brought them over to us. "These are on In-die," he said.

"Thanks," we said.

"Who's Indie?" Todd asked.

The bartender pointed. "The little guy with the date," he said. "He runs the place."

I turned to Mario. "Take it back," I said.

He clanked his glass against mine. "Fine, I take it back. She has great dog connections. But she's still not going to the wedding, so don't even think about it."

I took a sip of my wine. "She's got another commitment anyway," I said.

"Speaking of dates," Mario said, "where's yours?"

I still held out hope that I'd soften up Sean Ryan at the college fair and talk him into coming with me to the wedding. "Tied to my bedpost," I said. "I don't like to let him out at night."

"Never mind," Mario said. He leaned toward me and lowered his voice. "Guess what? Todd and I saw Mom and Dad coming out of the same hotel room."

"So what," I said. "That doesn't necessarily mean anything."

Mario turned to Todd. "See," he said. "I told you it didn't have to mean anything."

"Of course it does," Todd said.

Mario and I looked at each other. "Gross," we both said.

Todd smiled. "How old are you two?"

I looked around for Cannoli. She and Indie were curled up together under my chair. "As far as our parents are concerned, I think we're forever frozen at seven and eight." I took another sip of my wine. "They could have at least given us some warning."

"You know Mom," Mario said. "Her favorite saying is, 'That's why they call it a personal life.' "

"Ohmigod, that's exactly what she said to me at the airport." I shook my head. "It just makes me so sad. I mean, imagine if they get back together, and we had to go through all that for nothing. Back and forth from house to house, never sure where you'd left your favorite sweater or school book."

"That room I had at Mom's," Mario said. "It was like a shoe box."

"At least you had your own room," I said. "Angela and I were packed into that rickety bunk bed like sardines."

"Or," Todd said, "you could be happy for them that they found each other again."

Mario and I both rolled our eyes.

"So," Todd said. "Changing the subject. Did Mario tell you we had dinner with the Hairhouse guys?"

"Cut it out," I said. "What'd you do, smoke a peace pipe?"

"Pretty much," Mario said. "They're nice guys. No way are they trying to run us out of business. And they swore up and down they weren't the ones who called in the complaint about our septic system."

The bartender came over and placed a

bowl of peanuts on the bar in front of us.

"So," I said, once he'd walked away. "You haven't even told me how the wedding rehearsal went."

"Not bad," Mario said. "Except for the part where Tulia looked away for a second and Myles swallowed Andrew's ring."

27

"He ate the ring?" Sean Ryan asked.

"Yup," I said. "Only in my family. Apparently, everybody had been joking about it earlier in front of him. Myles has great comic timing, so he waited until he was supposed to hand Andrew's ring to Amy, then he gulped it down and toddled away."

"What were his parents doing?"

"I don't know about Mike, but Tulia was probably doing her nails. She's a bit of a train wreck."

The Georgia International Convention Center was back out by the airport. We'd taken 85 South from midtown in another Prius, this time a gray one with Georgia plates.

"I don't get it," I said. "Don't you at least want to drive a gas guzzler once in a while, just for the sake of variety? It's kind of creepy that you'd rent the same kind of car that you own."

Sean Ryan smiled. "How do you know I rented it?"

"Well, if you bought it for the weekend, then that's really creepy."

The GICC was huge and ultramodern. It was plopped in the middle of what seemed like a pretty seedy area to me, but the building itself looked safe enough, and it had plenty of parking. We found the exhibit hall right away and got our table set up in half the time it took us in Rhode Island.

"So, then what happened?" Sean Ryan asked as soon as he came back with two cups of coffee. "Are you sure you don't want something to eat?"

"No, I can wait." He handed me my coffee, and I ignored the little jolt when our fingers brushed. "Thanks. Okay, Mack and Maggie, their other kids, went out to dinner with everybody else, and Tulia and Mike took Myles to the emergency room to get his stomach x-rayed."

He sat down in his chair and took a sip of his coffee. "Did they have to operate?"

"Nah. The emergency room doctor just looked at the X-ray and asked what time the wedding was. Then he said, 'Well, I expect we'll be fixin' to see that ring just in the nick of time then.' "

Sean Ryan let out a big laugh. "That's

great. And how's your other nephew feeling about wearing that ring?"

"Andrew? He thinks it's hilarious. He told Tulia to tell Myles not to feel any pressure, that he could always borrow someone else's ring just for the ceremony."

"Good attitude."

"Yeah, he's a good kid. Anyway, when I left, they were all fighting about who got to do the hair and makeup for the bridal party."

"Must be great to have such a big family," Sean Ryan said.

"Most of the time." I took a sip of my coffee. "So, what's your family like?"

"Small. Both parents gone. One sister, a brother-in-law, two nephews. Think *Leave It to Beaver.* My ex and I used to call them the Connecticut Cleavers, though looking back, I think that was jealousy talking."

I took another sip of my coffee. "What do you mean?"

He shrugged. "We tried for a long time to have kids of our own, but it just never happened. Anyway, we'd started the adoption conversation, and suddenly we realized we couldn't stand each other. I think our house of cards just collapsed."

"That's too bad." I crossed one leg over the other, then uncrossed them again. "Do you still want kids?" popped out of my mouth before I thought it through.

He smiled. "Who knows? Probably, but I don't spend a lot of time thinking about it these days."

"Do you see them a lot?" I asked. "The Cleavers, I mean."

"Not as much as I used to when I was married. We get together for Thanksgiving, maybe a couple more times during the year."

Sean Ryan stood up and walked to the front of our table. He opened a box and started unloading his kits. This college fair was so much like the one in Rhode Island, it was giving me a major case of déjà vu. College banners were draped in front of rows and rows of tablecloth-covered booths. Tweedy people were setting up piles of brochures and applications and arranging displays of bottled water with the college names printed on them. There was a massage station, a manicure station, an ultracaffeinated drinks station, a safe sumo wrestling ring with bright yellow ropes.

I looked around. "You know, it's almost like a traveling circus. Everybody must just pack up their tents and head to the next college fair."

"It's big business," Sean Ryan said.

"Speaking of which," I said, "let me show you my new and revised kit."

I gave him the whole tour, piece by piece, explaining the changes I'd made and why I'd made them. "So, essentially," I said, "now it can work either with or without me actually being there."

He kept nodding his head the whole time I was talking. "It's brilliant," he said when I finished. "You put your finger on exactly what wasn't working, and refined it until it did. Most people can't do that, you know."

I tucked everything back into the kit I had disassembled and zipped it up again. "Well, I hope you haven't been under the illusion that I'm anything like most people," I said.

"Not for a minute," he said. We looked at each other, then he looked away. We both reached for our coffee. "Okay, what's next?" he asked.

"Well," I said. "My Web site's up, and I've submitted it to a bunch of search engines. I've made up ten percent–off coupons to give to our salon clients. And I was wondering about trying to get on one of the local television shows. Maybe *Beantown*? I've done hair and makeup for some of those guests."

"Do you know the name of the guest booker?"

"Yeah. Karen something or other."

"I'll give her a call on Monday," Sean Ryan said casually.

"You know how to book a show?" I asked.

He grinned. "If I already knew how to do it, it wouldn't be half as much fun. I'll let you know what happens."

I decided to go for it, but first I needed ammunition. I unscrewed a pot of a blood-red Nars lip lacquer called Bewitched and slowly rubbed some on my lips. I could feel Sean Ryan watching my every stroke. I looked up and into his eyes. Maybe being in the South was starting to rub off on me, because I even batted my eyelashes a little. "I don't get it," I said. "You'll try to get me on a TV show, but you won't even come to one itsy-bitsy wedding with me? Come on, someone has to help me keep an eye out for okra."

Sean Ryan crossed his arms over his chest. "We've already had this conversation, Bella. I don't want to hurt your feelings, but I'm not interested in taking things further."

The doors opened, and everyone poured in all at once. I slid as far as I could to the opposite end of the table. I angled my body so that I was facing away from Sean Ryan and got to work.

We both had huge lines right away, even

though he was giving the guidance counselor's kits away for free, and I was making sure I collected every cent. Some people only had credit cards, so I held their kits hostage while they found an ATM.

I smiled. I flattered. I mixed their custom foundation. I wrote down product suggestions for them. I tucked everything into a Bella's Bag of Beauty Basics kit and handed it over. I went on to the next person in line. And the whole time I fumed. *I'm not interested in taking things further.* It wasn't like I was even looking for a real date, just someone to hang out with at a wedding. What a pompous ass.

Finally, I sold my last kit. I stretched. I looked over at the table next to ours. I smiled at the bored-looking guy standing there in front of a pile of college applications.

"Having fun yet?" he asked.

I laughed like he'd said something witty.

He held a custom-printed water bottle out to me. "Here you go," he said. "Hot in here."

I batted my eyelashes. "Aren't you just the sweetest thing," I said in what I hoped passed for a Southern accent.

Sean Ryan made a disgusted sound behind me.

I looked down at the insignia on the label. "Wow, Emory. Great school. How long have you been working there?"

As the guy took a deep breath and got ready to tell me the story of his life, a sumo wrestler in big white diapers walked by, heading for the wrestling ring. "Now that looks like fun," I said. "I've always wanted to try safe sumo wrestling."

"Let's go," the guy said.

"Sure," I said.

Sean Ryan stood up. "Excuse me," he said. "But the lady's wrestling card is full."

The guy shrugged.

I stood up. "Excuse me," I said. "But where do you get off telling me who I can and cannot wrestle with?"

Sean Ryan raised an eyebrow. "How many times have I tried to get you to try that? I thought you said you didn't want to."

I put both hands on my hips. "I thought you said you weren't *interested in taking things further.*"

Sean Ryan rolled up the cloth banner and tablecloth he'd brought and tucked them into a cardboard box, along with the e-mail list he'd collected for follow-up. He grabbed my shoulder bag.

"Hey," I said. "Where do you think you're going with that?"

"Come on," he said. "Unless you're chicken."

"I am so not chicken," I said.

I don't know how much Sean Ryan paid the guy in the diapers to get us front cuts, but he pulled us right between the ropes and into the wrestling ring. Since we were in the South, everybody was too polite to start screaming at us like they would have in Boston.

I was totally going to kick Sean Ryan's butt. I glared at him while a father and son stepped out of their gigantic sumo wrestling suits. I glared at him some more while they took off helmets shaped like traditional sumo hairstyles, complete with little black vinyl topknots.

Sean Ryan held up the two enormous vinyl suits. "Red or blue?" he asked.

"Whatever," I said.

He held out the blue suit.

"Red," I said.

The suits were truly massive. They were vaguely flesh-colored, maybe a MAC NC30 or so, and filled with so much air and foam they pretty much stood up on their own. The colored wrestling belts were attached to them, and they had attached neck pads, too.

We held on to the bright yellow ropes of

the sumo wrestling ring while we stepped into our suits. The guy in diapers helped us pull them up over our shoulders. As soon as I let go of the rope, I started to tip over.

"Whoa," I said. I grabbed the rope again.

"Weebles wobble but they don't fall down," Sean Ryan said. "Remember that?"

"Oh, grow up," I said.

The guy in diapers pointed at the red mat, which took up most of the ring. It had a large blue circle in the center. "Stand in blue. Bell ring. Push each other out. Step on red, other guy win."

Belatedly, I remembered I'd never liked organized sports. Before I had time to say anything, like *how do you get out of this suit,* the bell rang. Sean Ryan pushed himself off the ropes and staggered into the middle. I held on tight. Sean Ryan flapped his arms like a giant sumo chicken and yelled something at me that I couldn't hear. I let go. I grabbed the rope again. The diaper guy walked over to me.

"Wait," I said.

He didn't. He gave me a big push. I staggered until my sumo stomach collided with Sean Ryan's. We bounced off each other and both wobbled a few steps backward. He caught his balance and staggered in my direction until we made contact again. This time I fell back, all the way to the mat, and he landed on top of me.

Our padded vinyl stomachs worked just like a giant seesaw. His feet went up in the air, and his mouth tilted down to mine. We were like two beached whales, and then somehow we were kissing.

He was a great kisser, even in a full-body vinyl suit. He tasted like coffee. I caught the faint scent of coconut, which was either his Paul Mitchell Extra-Body Sculpting Foam, or someone in the audience was drinking a piña colada.

We both leaned in the same direction at once, and we started to roll. We rolled over and over, picking up momentum until we crashed into the ropes on the side of the ring.

"Holy cannoli," Sean Ryan said, his lips still inches from mine.

"Awkward," I said. "But oddly hot."

The crowd began to clap and cheer. "Ohmigod," I said. "I hope that's not for us."

"Come on," Sean Ryan said. "Let's get out of here."

I leaned back in the passenger seat of the Prius and fluffed up my hair. "Boyohboy," I said. "It sure doesn't take long to get helmet hair, does it?"

"Listen," Sean Ryan said. "I'm sorry I kissed you."

I stopped fluffing. "Gee, thanks."

"Can I finish?"

I nodded.

"Okay, I've got two things to tell you. One, I was in love with a married woman once. She went back to her husband. I think I knew all along she was going to, but I put a lot of time and effort into trying to convince us both that she wouldn't. I don't ever want to go through that again. So, you want to hang out, work on your kit, whatever, I'm in. But, that's it."

Every bit of the hurt showed in Sean Ryan's hazel eyes. I didn't think I'd ever go back to Craig, but then again, until recently I didn't think I'd ever sleep with him again either.

"Okay," I said. I put my hand on top of Sean Ryan's. "Geesh, who made life so complicated anyway?"

He pulled my hand toward him and kissed it lightly. We smiled at each other. "Thanks," he said.

"You're welcome," I said. "Okay, what's the other thing?"

He closed his eyes. "You know the condo people who've been trying to get their hands on your father's waterfront salon?"

I nodded.

He opened one eye. "Well, I'm one of the investors."

"What?"

"Yeah, well, you know, there's a group of us. We buy up waterfront property and develop it. High-end condos, as green as we can make them and still be cost-efficient. . . ."

"So, get out of it," I said.

"I can't. I have a commitment to the other investors. It's business. I shouldn't even be talking to you about it."

I flashed on Sean Ryan's waterfront house in North Marshbury. I wondered how much he'd paid off the poor old man who used to live there. "Ohmigod," I said. "You really are a barracuda."

"Hey, there's nothing wrong with buying property."

"Take me back to my hotel," I said. "I don't want to be late for my nephew's wedding."

Nobody said a word the whole way back. Sean Ryan pulled the Prius over to the curb in front of Hotel Indigo. "It's really not a bad thing," he said. "Your father stands to make a ton of money. And we offer fair market value."

"Yeah, right," I said. "Before or after you call the health inspector?"

"What?"

"You should be ashamed of yourself. Anyone who would call in a phony failed septic system is pond scum. Lower than pond scum. Do you know how much money it takes to put in a new one? And even if you have the money, how would you like a big grass-covered hump between you and your view?"

Sean Ryan wrinkled his forehead. "What are you talking about?"

I slammed the car door in his face.

28

I turned away from the car without looking back and stomped into the hotel. Cannoli and Indie were in the lobby, so I put them on their leashes and walked them a few blocks down Peachtree Street. I found a little froufrou doggie boutique and bought them each a treat, but I was too angry to enjoy the walk. We headed back to the hotel, and Indie came up to hang out while Cannoli and I got ready.

I took a scalding hot shower and scrubbed myself so hard with the washcloth I was lucky I had any skin left when I finished. I slathered myself with the whole little bottle of Aveda Replenishing Body Moisturizer I found in the bathroom to make up for it. I blow-dried my hair and made up my face. I put on my stupid pretty new dress.

I'd been planning to wear a bold red called Frankly Scarlett on my lips. I couldn't wait to tell everybody what it was called when they told me how great it looked. Instead, I rolled on a pinkish copper called Kiss My Lips. That wasn't the only thing Sean Ryan could kiss, as far as I was concerned.

I brought Cannoli into the bathroom, so she'd have some privacy from Indie, and helped her into her cornflower blue taffeta bubble bridesmaid dress. At least there was still a chance for canine love this weekend.

I was a little bit late getting to the lobby, where I probably could have hitched a ride to the wedding with someone in my family, so it looked like I'd have to find my own way to the church. The Hotel Indigo owners raved about Cannoli's dress, maybe because it was blue, and invited her to spend the night at their house. They promised to have her back at the hotel by checkout time. I thanked them and headed out to grab a cab.

"Good luck," one of them yelled after me. "I hope they found a priest who speaks Northern."

I found out what that meant soon enough. Catholic weddings with a full Mass are long enough, but Southern Catholic weddings with a full Mass are practically forever. Tulia turned around in her pew and flashed me a thumbs-up, so apparently things on the ring front had worked themselves out.

Maggie was adorable in her soft yellow dress with a big satin bow. She was clearly having a blast throwing yellow rose petals in front of her as she walked behind the other flower girls.

Andrew looked so handsome standing across from Mario and Todd. I tried to get a clear picture of Julie in my mind, and to think about what it would have meant to her to have lived to see her son get married, but all I could think about was how much Andrew had grown to look like Mario and Todd. His posture was just like Todd's, and he smiled exactly like Mario. I wondered if Lizzie, Luke, and I had spent enough time together that they sometimes reminded people of me.

Amy was gorgeous in a taffeta A-line dress with a beaded bodice. It had a pickup skirt, which made me think of the peaks on a lemon meringue pie. It was an unusual color, just the barest hint of gold, which I could never have worn, but it worked beautifully with her golden hair, blue eyes, and warm skin. Her bridesmaids had dresses in a deeper copper, and Mario and Todd and the groomsmen all had copper taffeta handkerchiefs in their tuxedo pockets.

I sighed. The ushers had seated me next

to Angela and her family, but I suddenly felt conspicuously alone. It didn't help that Sophia and Craig were in the pew ahead of me. The priest droned on and on, and I ignored him, something I'd been doing pretty much since I'd first set foot in a church. Angela's and Tulia's families went to church regularly, but the rest of us avoided it whenever possible. The Catholic Church felt the same way about most of us, so it seemed like we were even. I couldn't have been married in it even if I'd wanted to, since Craig was divorced. My father was divorced times three, and Mario was gay. We were lucky they hadn't stopped us at the door today.

My parents were sitting in the front row, just ahead of Tulia and Mike. They'd probably hate each other again by Monday, but I found myself holding my breath as I watched them. Sitting or standing, they leaned lightly against each other, hands clasped together. I wondered again what it would have been like if they had stayed together. I wondered if I'd ever meet someone I'd still be drawn to four decades later.

Mack and Myles were in miniature versions of the groomsmen outfits, each holding a ring on a copper taffeta pillow. Myles was rocking back and forth, watching his ring, then looking up at the people in the pews and grinning.

My stomach began to growl, and I started to wish I'd forced myself to eat at least a snack. Finally it was time for the vows. Andrew spoke up loud and clear, and Mario and Todd and the rest of us beamed at him. Amy did a great job, too, and I loved the way they both smiled a lot and looked like they weren't taking themselves too seriously.

Andrew nodded at Mack. Mack walked over and held his pillow up. Andrew bent over, pulled the ribbon that held the ring in place, and picked up the ring. He took Amy's hand. "I give you this ring," he said, "as a symbol of my love and faithfulness. As I place it on your finger, I commit my heart and soul to you."

My eyes teared up. One part of me wanted to believe they'd stay together forever. But the other part wanted to jump up on the seat of the pew and warn them. I mean, sure, they were in love now, but what were the chances a wedding ring was going to keep one of them from breaking the other's heart?

It was Amy's turn. She nodded at Myles.

Myles turned around and took off like a baby bat out of hell, running just as fast as his stubby little legs would carry him.

Everybody gasped, and the collective intake of breath filled the church.

"Mack, Maggie, I mean *Myles*," Tulia yelled.

Myles put his feet together and managed two-footed jumps down each of the three steps of the altar.

A few people let out sharp bursts of laughter. We were all standing on our tiptoes and leaning toward the aisle, so we wouldn't miss anything.

Myles started churning his legs again and headed down the center aisle.

My father leaned out of his pew and caught him as he toddled by. He held Myles up in the air over his head while we all cheered. My father passed him over to my mother, then tried to take the pillow out of his hand. Myles let out a bloodcurdling scream. My mother whispered something in his ear. He let go.

My father held the copper taffeta pillow at waist height. He took his time, walking up to the altar in an exaggerated step together, step together. He climbed the three stairs the same way.

When he came to Amy, he knelt down on one knee, bowed his shiny bald head, and extended the pillow.

Everybody burst into applause.

The thing about my father is that he never knows when to quit. He stayed on the altar until the priest pronounced Andrew and Amy husband and wife and told Andrew he could now kiss the bride.

As soon as they finished kissing, my father yelled, "Wait!"

Shoulders back, he glided down the three steps of the altar and headed straight for my mother. He knelt down just outside her pew. He reached for her hand. He bowed his shiny bald head.

"Mary Margaret O'Neill," he said in a voice that filled the church. *"Ti amo. Mi vuoi sposare?"* Just to make sure nobody missed anything, he translated. "I love you. Will you marry me?"

My mother kept one firm hand on Myles and used the other one to help my father to his feet. "That's enough, Larry," she said. "Let the kids have their day."

"Did you hear that?" my father roared. "She didn't say no!"

The Margaret Mitchell House was a great place for a wedding reception. Guests milled around a charming courtyard with a sunken garden and drifted onto covered porches and into parlor rooms. Waitstaff wearing tuxedo pants and crisp white shirts walked around with appetizers on small round trays.

A waiter stopped in front of us and extended his tray.

"That doesn't have any okra in it, does it?" I asked.

"No, Ma'am, it doesn't. Beef, pork sausage, cheese, and spices. It's called Hanky Panky."

"Well," I said, "then I'd better take two, since it might be the only shot I get."

The waiter laughed politely, then handed me a napkin that read *Amy and Andrew.* "Sir?" he said.

"No thanks," Mario said. "How about a drink, Sis? Maybe it'll loosen your tongue."

I'd been thinking things through, and I finally figured out what the row of turkeys that had crossed in front of me right after I'd slept with Craig meant. Not Craig is a turkey. *All men are turkeys.* "Well," I said, "this calls for a toast. I think I'll have a Wild Turkey. Maybe even a whole flock."

Mario ordered a glass of wine, and the waiter tiptoed away. Another waiter came by with a tray, and Mario took a shrimp and dipped it in a little bowl of cocktail sauce.

"No, thanks," I said. "I'm still working on my Hanky Panky."

"Out with it," Mario said. "What happened to your date? He's not still tied to your bedpost, is he?"

"Nah, he escaped," I said. "Just as well. He was showing signs of wear and tear anyway."

"Sorry it didn't work out," Mario said.

I shrugged. We both started watching our parents, who were sitting close together on a garden bench. We heard our father retelling the story of how he saved the day, and watched our mother nodding and smiling along.

"Geez," I said. "I mean, it's not like she missed any of it. She was right next to him."

Angela came over to stand with us. "It's unbelievable," she said. "When did that start?" I could tell she was holding her breath when she looked at them, too.

"My first sighting was in the hotel," Mario said. "Todd and I saw them coming out of the same room together, heading for breakfast."

"Not to be competitive, but I was on to them way before that," I said. "At Logan, before we even boarded."

"Show-off," Mario said.

"What can I say," I said. "I'm good."

Angela grabbed a shrimp off the tray as it

318

came by. "Couldn't they have just stayed together the first time around?"

29

"A drink, *amore mio?*" Lucky Larry Shaughnessy, our father, asked our mother, Mary Margaret O'Neill. He had loosened his tie, and you could just see the thick gold chain of his *cornicello* peeking out from his collar.

"When in Rome," our mother said. They smiled at each other. "As long as it's not that awful grappa."

Our father sauntered away in his single-breasted red-and-white-striped seersucker suit. It was hard to tell which was shinier, his scalp or his white bucks.

Our mother turned around and saw us staring at her. "Uh-oh," I said. "Here she comes."

"How lovely to be out in a garden at night," she said. She was wearing a long flowing dress with silver threads that matched her hair and sparkled when the outdoor lights caught them. "What a spectacular wedding." She leaned over and kissed Mario. "You must be so proud."

We all stared at her. "What?" she said.

"Nothing," we said.

She shrugged. "He picked up the phone a month ago and invited me to be his date for the wedding. It took a lot of *cogliones* to do that."

"What's that mean?" Angela asked.

"Balls," my mother said.

"But you hate him," Angela said.

"Our whole childhood was based on that," I said.

"If you'd stayed together, I might have been more popular," Angela said.

"I might have turned out straight," Mario said, and we all burst out laughing.

"Are you going to marry him?" Angela asked.

My mother tilted her head and shrugged. "I'm taking it one date at a time. But bottom line, if I only had six months to live, I'd have the most fun with your father."

"Maybe you should wait for the diagnosis," I said.

Mario kissed our mother on the cheek. "Enjoy every minute," he said. "By the way, what did you say to Myles in the church to make him let go of the pillow?"

She smiled. "I just started counting. It

works every time. I don't think I ever made it past five with any of you."

"Yay, team!" Angela cheered, and we all reached for one another and had a group hug, just to humor her. It wasn't her fault she was such a soccer mom.

We dropped our arms and took a step back but stayed in our circle.

When I turned around, Sean Ryan was talking to my father.

My heart started to beat like crazy. I took a deep breath. I reminded myself that all men are turkeys, which only reminded me of something even more pressing: That waiter still hadn't shown up with my Wild Turkey.

"Excuse me," I said to my family. "But I think I need a drink."

That waiter wasn't easy to find, so I headed for the bar and ordered another one. Straight up.

I was in a shot glass kind of mood, but the bartender put it in a brandy snifter, which took some of the fun out of it, in my opinion. "Here you go, little lady," he said.

"Gobble gobble," I said, before I took a healthy slug. I started to cough.

My former husband came out of nowhere to pat me on the back.

"Thanks," I said. I put my drink on the

bar and reached for my clutch. Maybe I'd put on some Frankly Scarlett after all.

"What is that anyway?" Craig asked. "You don't drink hard liquor."

"Wild Turkey," I said. "Why? What's it to you?"

Craig smiled. He was wearing a suit I'd never seen before. "Be careful. Did you eat anything yet?"

"Not your problem," I said.

I smelled his Paul Mitchell Extra-Body Sculpting Foam before I saw him. "Can I talk to you for a minute?" Sean Ryan asked.

Craig held out his hand and introduced himself. "You look familiar," he added.

"Sean," Sean Ryan said. "I think we've seen each other at the salon."

Sophia walked up to us. Craig introduced her. We all stood there awkwardly for a moment or two. I tried to decide which was worse, standing around with my former and his present, who was somehow still my half sister, or being alone with the guy I'd thought might be my future until he'd decided he didn't want to take things further, even though for some unknown reason he'd shown up anyway. Life was way too confusing. No wonder I needed a drink. I picked up my glass from the bar and took another long gobble. It went down a lot smoother this time.

When I looked up again, Sophia was giving me a funny look. For a moment I wondered if Craig had admitted to her that we'd slept together, but I knew all too well that wasn't his style. My sister shorthand kicked in, and an actual chill came over me as I read Sophia's expression: *There's nothing you can do to stop me from coming on to this guy either.* She tossed her hair and smiled a killer smile. "Your new boyfriend is really cute," she said.

I handed my glass to Sean Ryan. "Keep an eye on the turkey for me," I said. "We'll be right back."

I grabbed Sophia by the arm.

"Ouch," she said.

I dragged her into a small bathroom and locked the door. "Listen," I said. "You're my sister, and you're embarrassing me. You're embarrassing yourself."

She leaned back against the sink. "Half sister," she said.

"It doesn't matter," I said. "You're still my sister. I've loved you your whole life, since the minute you were born."

She began to cry. I put my arms around her and held her while she sobbed, the way I used to when she was little and somebody had been mean to her at school or some boy had broken her heart.

"Why'd you do it?" I asked. "At what point did you actually say to yourself, 'This is my sister and I'm going to sleep with her husband'?"

"You weren't paying any attention to him," she mumbled into my shoulder. "I guess I didn't think you wanted him anymore."

I pushed her away. "That's bullshit," I said. "You did it because you've always wanted everything I have. I love you, but get over it. Stay with Craig, or don't. I don't even care anymore. But get your act together, Sophia, or I don't want you in my life."

I left her in the bathroom and went back to the bar. "Down the hall, last room on the right," I said to Craig.

"But —" he said.

"Go," I said.

"But —" he said again.

"Frankly, Craig," I said, "I don't give a damn."

Sean Ryan raised an eyebrow after he was gone.

"Somebody had to say it eventually," I said.

"You okay?" Sean Ryan asked.

"Never been better," I said. He handed

me my Wild Turkey. "Do you think you can trade this in for a chardonnay?" I asked.

"Sure," he said. "If you'll take a walk with me."

We found some chairs on the far corner of the lawn, tucked beside some hedges, not far from the street.

"Okay, what," I said.

He laughed. "You're such a charmer."

"Look who's talking," I said.

"I spoke to your father," he said.

Even with the outdoor lighting, I couldn't quite see his eyes, but I knew they were hazel with flecks of gold. "I saw," I said.

"I didn't know anything about that call to the health inspector. I've already pulled out of the group. And I told them to back off, or I'd tell your father who made the call."

"They'd never get a haircut in that town again" was all I could think to say. A piece of the puzzle was still missing, but I couldn't quite put my finger on it.

"I would have done it, even if he wasn't your father. Calling in a failed septic system is playing dirty. These old systems almost always fail, and he'll have to put in a new one. It's going to cost your father some good money."

I didn't say anything.

"Even if he can afford it, what if he couldn't? People lose their homes over things like this every day. I don't do business that way."

I still didn't say anything.

"And there's not a lot of land for the system, so I don't know what it would do to the property aesthetically. I told him I'd do some research for him. There are some new compact septic tanks. They have to be pumped more often, but they take up a lot less space."

I was too curious not to ask. "What did he say?"

Sean Ryan smiled. "He took me up on it. And he tried to get me to pay for the whole system. What a character." He reached for my hand. "So, are we okay now?"

I stood up. "No, you and my father are okay. *We're* not okay."

"What?"

I chugged down the rest of my wine. "It's all about business for you, isn't it? Well, let me tell you, I have no intention of pursuing even a friendship with someone who thinks business is more important than I am."

I was halfway down the street before I realized that, since it was my nephew's wedding, I shouldn't have been the one to leave.

I should have made Sean Ryan leave. It was too late now, since it would ruin my exit if I went back. I wondered how far it was to Hotel Indigo. I wondered if I was walking in the right direction. It was hard to tell. It was dark. I was in a strange city. And as much as I tried to fight them, hot tears were stinging my eyes.

Sean Ryan pulled up in a no parking zone in his gray Prius and rolled down the passenger window. I kept walking. He inched the car along beside me.

"Come on," he said. "At least let me drive you back to your hotel. It's not safe."

"I'll take my chances," I said. I picked up my pace.

So did he. "Please?" he said. He leaned across the passenger seat. "I have crime statistics."

"How bad?" I asked. A guy walking in my direction suddenly looked armed and dangerous.

Sean Ryan pulled around an illegally parked van, and I lost sight of him.

"Well," he said, when he came back into view, "things are definitely moving in the right direction, but there's still a ways to go before it's safe to walk at night."

I stepped off the curb, grabbed the door handle, and pulled. "Fine," I said. "Just don't talk to me, okay?"

He waited until I was buckled, then we merged with the traffic.

"You're right," Sean Ryan said. "I should have talked to you first. I should have told you you're more important to me than any business deal."

I looked straight ahead. "I would have liked it if you'd said that. I would have even told you that I'm never ever going back to Craig. Ever."

We looked at each other.

"I still think we should just be friends," Sean Ryan said. "Maybe work on your kit for a while, see how it goes."

"You're such a control freak. That's what this is, you know. You can't find a place and freeze it. Life doesn't stop. It moves on."

"Thank you for the pearls of wisdom," he said.

"You're welcome," I said.

He reached over and held my hand. I slid over to his side as far as the Prius would allow. I closed my eyes and let in the magic of the moment.

"Any other pithy advice for me?"

I thought about it. "Yes," I said. "You can try to avoid getting hurt six ways from Sunday, but it still might happen. And don't you dare ever sleep with one of my sisters.

Or my brother."

Sean Ryan put on his blinker. He pulled over to the side of the road and put the car into park. There's nothing like a good kiss in a Prius.

30

"It's good," I said. "But it's not quite the same without that sumo suit."

"Maybe I can find a couple around here somewhere," he said. "Do you want me to check?"

"Don't you dare go anywhere," I said.

He rolled us over across the width of his king-size bed. I pushed back, and we rolled back over in the other direction.

"Show-off," we both said at once.

Morning sex with Sean Ryan was seriously fun, but it was getting late, and eventually one of us was going to have to make a move to get up. We both stared up at the ceiling. I was happy to note I'd ended up on the right side of the bed. "I can't believe you didn't tell me you owned a loft in Atlanta. Not to mention another Prius."

He propped himself up on an elbow and kissed me on my shoulder. "What? So you

331

could try to sleep with me to get to the Prius?"

"I've been plotting it for months, you salon stalker you," I said. "Hey, what's the name of this place anyway?"

"Peachtree Lofts."

"What else?"

I'd been otherwise occupied kissing Sean Ryan, so I hadn't been paying too much attention last night, but I vaguely remembered underground parking and a lobby that looked like a modern art museum. His apartment had exposed ductwork on the ceiling and an exposed brick wall behind the bed. He had leather furniture and some nice art on the walls, and not much clutter.

"So, what," I said, "are you obnoxiously rich or something?"

He laughed. "No. It was just a great investment. I bought it for practically nothing in 1995, when they first turned it into condos. It used to house the CDC, the Center for Disease Control, back when it was still called the Center for Infectious Diseases."

"I hoped you scrubbed it with bleach first."

"After that, it housed the Department of Agriculture, so maybe you'll just get mad cow disease."

"Great."

"Anyway, I kept it because it's everything my house in Marshbury isn't. It's a nice balance."

I pulled the sheets up over my shoulders. The comforter had ended up on the floor somehow.

He sat up in bed. "How about some breakfast? There's a great place down the street called The Flying Biscuit."

I pulled the sheet over my head. "I'm not leaving," I said. "Ever."

"Any particular reason?"

I'd spent some time thinking about this last night, after I'd dozed off and then woken up again. "The minute we leave this loft," I said, "everything's going to get all messed up again."

Sean Ryan slid under and pulled the sheet over his head, too. He stretched his legs up in the air and held the sheet up with his feet like a tent. I put my feet up there, too, to make the tent bigger.

"See," I said. "We can just stay here and pretend we're camping. Toast some marshmallows, tell some ghost stories. Watch your unibrow grow back."

He walked one of his feet over until it was touching mine. "Would it help if I recited your speech of last night back to you? I could start with the part about being a control freak."

"I was just trying to get you into bed," I said.

"Ha. Not to rush this along, but are your legs starting to shake yet?"

We kicked the tent down and sat up. "We have air-conditioning," I said. "And water. We'll be fine."

"You haven't seen my refrigerator. We'll die of starvation in no time."

"Okay," I said. "I'll go, but don't say I didn't warn you."

I jumped in the shower first, while Sean Ryan made coffee. There is nothing in the world like a cup of coffee you didn't have to make yourself. It was rich and strong, and I drank it, wearing his robe, a fresh coat of Afterglow on my lips, looking out the window, trying not to think.

He came out of the bathroom with a towel wrapped around his waist. My heart did a little leap in my chest.

"Hey," he said.

"Hey," I said. I could feel us slipping away from each other already.

He poured himself a cup of coffee, then leaned back against the kitchen counter. "Listen, why don't you just stay here for the week and fly back to Boston with me on

Friday? I have plenty of frequent flyer miles. Can you juggle your clients? Or get someone to cover for you?"

My cell phone rang in my shoulder bag, which had somehow ended up on the floor by the front door. I got up, found my phone, and looked at it. "It's Mario," I said. "I'd better answer it."

"Esther Williams died," he said as soon as I said hello.

"Oh, no," I said.

"She left a list of final requests. She wants you to do her hair and makeup."

"No way," I said. "You know I don't do corpses."

Sean Ryan followed me into his bedroom. "Not to pry," he said. "But did I just hear you say you don't do corpses?"

I was already pulling yesterday's dress over my head. "I knew it," I said. "We didn't even have to leave the apartment. Everything always gets screwed up. People get hurt. People break up with you. People die. It's not even worth . . . Oh, just forget it."

Sean Ryan put an arm around me. I slid out from under it and bent down to pick up my shoes.

"Do you think breakfast might help?" he asked.

I shook my head. "Just take me back to

the hotel, okay?"

Cannoli and I caught an early evening flight back to Logan, and I spent a sleepless night in my apartment. When I got to the funeral home the next morning, Sophia was waiting for me in the parking lot. We both locked our cars and started heading for the back door. My stomach was in knots already.

"Thanks," I said. "Did Mario make you come?"

"No," she said. "I wanted to."

Sophia rang the doorbell, and a man opened the door for us. "Come on in, girls," he said. "She's waiting for you in the embalming room."

I wanted to turn and run just like Myles did at the wedding, but I forced myself to keep breathing, to keep walking. O'Donohue's Funeral Home was set in an old Victorian, with rich wood floors and intricate carved moldings, but the embalming room was cold and sterile. It had stainless steel shelves, a huge stainless steel sink, and a drain in the middle of a white tile floor.

I shivered as we walked in. Esther Williams was already in her casket. She'd clearly picked it out herself. The wood was ornately carved and stained avocado green, and it was lined with a soft pink crepe. There was a darker pink rose embroidered on the lining of the lid. Right now it faced out into the room, but you could tell it was positioned so that when the casket was closed, the rose would end up right over her nose.

I'd been hoping I'd be able to use my airbrush gun, so I didn't have to touch her much, at least for the foundation, but I was afraid I'd mess up that lining. I pulled out the legs on my makeup case and set it up on the floor next to the casket. My hands were shaking.

Esther Williams was wearing a hot pink dress, one she'd worn to the salon about a million times. It was tight and cut low, and she called it her husband-hunting dress. Salon de Lucio wasn't going to be the same without her. I just couldn't believe she was dead. She had always been one of the most alive people I knew, sparkling with vitality and true beauty, the kind that bubbles to the surface from the inside.

I must have been standing there for a while, because Sophia said, "Here, I'll start." She reached into my case and pulled out a triangular foam sponge. She placed a finger on a round black MAC Studio Tech foundation compact. "What is she, an

NW25?"

I nodded. Sophia spread the foundation on gently, lovingly, covering not just Esther Williams's face, but her neck and cleavage, and the tops of her hands.

"How do you stand it?" I asked.

"It's not so bad," Sophia said. "I just pretend it's me, and I think about how I'd want to look good if so many people were going to be staring at me."

I rummaged in my case until I located my curling iron. I found an outlet under one of the shelves and plugged it in.

"Some places," Sophia said, "they put the caskets up higher and tell you just to do the half of the face that shows. Same with the hair."

"Oh, that's awful," I said. "She'd hate that. We have to do all of her."

"I always do," Sophia said. "That's how Dad taught Mario and me."

"I was such a chicken," I said. "I was always so jealous when one of you got to go with Dad when he had a body to do, but not quite jealous enough to go." I took a deep breath. "Okay, I'm good. I'll take it from here."

I set the foundation with a large brush and some loose opaque powder to make sure it lasted through both the wake and the funeral. Then I added some MAC powder blush in Angel, which now I knew really did look good on everybody, even dead bodies.

I could almost hear Esther Williams saying, "Okay, now give me some eyes." I pulled out a shelf in my case and lined up everything I'd need to give her some unforgettable eyes. Almay color cream eye shadow in Mocha Shimmer, Bobbi Brown longwear gel eyeliner in Black Ink and NYC self-adhesive eyelashes. Plus Maybelline Great Lash mascara in Very Black.

I placed a tube of Revlon Super Lustrous Lipstick in Gentlemen Prefer Pink on the shelf for my final touch. If there were husbands to be had in her next life, I wanted her to find one right away. I took a deep breath. I picked up a disposable foam eye shadow brush and dipped it in the Mocha Shimmer. I braced one hand on the edge of the casket. I reached for Esther Williams's eyelid.

When I touched it, it moved.

I screamed. And screamed.

"What happened?" Sophia asked calmly when I stopped.

"It moved," I whispered. "Her eyelid moved."

"Don't worry," Sophia said. "It's just wax.

They must have had to rebuild part of her face." She walked over and touched the eyelid lightly, then ran her finger along the lower lip. "Look, this is wax, too. She might have fallen when she had the heart attack. Or thrown up, and it took them a while to find the body. Sometimes the acid . . ."

I turned around and vomited into the stainless steel sink, then I went outside to wait for Sophia.

Sophia handed me my makeup case. "You okay?" she asked.

"Fine," I said. I was sitting on the ground, leaning back against a sugar maple tree on the edge of the parking lot. When I moved my feet, the first dead leaves of the season made a dry, rustling sound. "Thanks."

"Don't worry," Sophia said. "She looks great."

"I'll take your word for it."

Sophia smiled. "You want me to follow you back to your place?"

I shook my head. "I'll be okay to drive in a minute."

She slid down to the ground next to me. I moved over so she could lean back against the tree, too.

"Craig's moving back into his condo in Boston," Sophia said. "The tenant's lease is up this weekend."

I didn't say anything.

"It was his idea, but I think I would have broken up with him anyway. You're much more fun to hang out with."

"Yeah," I said. "Especially today."

"I'm sorry," Sophia said. "I'm really sorry."

I put my arm around her, and she rested her head on my shoulder. "Do you regret not having kids of your own?" she asked.

"I'm not sure. I know I regret letting Craig make the decision for me."

Sophia sighed. "Mario's going to start sending me to New York. He's got an in for per-diem work at one of the networks. He and Todd say Boston's such a tiny market, and they want to expand. They're talking about Atlanta, too."

"That's great. It'll be good for you to broaden your horizons." I took my arm back and pushed myself up to a standing position. "Listen," I said. "The truth is, I didn't think I could forgive you, but I forgive you. I love you. But if you ever do anything like that again . . ."

"I won't," Sophia said. "I promise." She stood up, too. She gave me a hug.

I turned my head, so she wouldn't have to smell my breath. A green Prius pulled into the parking lot. My heart started beating like crazy, but my head knew there was more than one green Prius in Marshbury.

Sean Ryan pulled up beside me and rolled down the window.

"Those things have power windows?" I said. "That seems like a real waste of energy."

Sophia waved over her shoulder as she walked away. "I'm not even going to look at him," she said.

Sean Ryan put his car into park and climbed out. "Do you want to try that greeting again? Maybe something like, 'How nice of you to fly back early to make sure I was okay'?"

"Thank you," I said.

"So listen," he said. "I can't promise you I won't die, but it's probably not going to happen today, so why don't we just try to keep a positive attitude here."

I'd actually been thinking the same thing myself. I mean, maybe if the right person floats into your life, you have to jump in with both feet and try to make it work before the tide turns.

"I agree," I said.

"Well, that's a first."

I smiled. "Hey, life goes fast. Before we know it, we'll both be lying there in a casket, hoping to get makeup on both sides of our faces."

Sean Ryan raised a well-groomed eyebrow. "That's your idea of positive?"

I was trying to stay downwind, but he took a step toward me. I put a hand up to cover my mouth. In a perfect world, my nostrils would be filled with the smell of his Paul Mitchell Extra-Body Sculpting Foam and not embalming fluid. My breath would be fresh, and I'd have Nars Eros on my lips, which would shimmer a raspberry rose in the setting sun.

"Boyohboy, could I use a toothbrush," I said.

"I could follow you to your place and wait while you brush."

I looked at him. He looked at me. "Positively," I said.

31

I had to stand on my tiptoes to take down the SUMMER BLOWOUT sign. I cleaned the big picture window at the front of the salon with Windex and a paper towel first, because Mario was watching. Then I unfurled the FALL FOIL SPECIAL sign I'd designed and taped it up in the same place.

I stepped back to see how it looked. I took a deep breath of crisp autumn air.

Mario came out to join me. "How's it look?" I asked.

He barely glanced at it. "Nice," he said. "But listen to this. I think you might have reeled in a big one."

It had been a crazy week. Sean Ryan managed to get me on *Beantown.* Somebody at DailyCandy saw me on the show, and they'd sent a Today's Candy e-mail about my kit not just to their Boston list, but also to every major city in the country. My Web site was hopping, and Mario was helping me stay on top of all the orders.

"That's great," I said. "Who?"

"One of Miley Cyrus's people e mailed. They want to talk to you about doing a custom foundation for her, and maybe even designing a new look."

"I can do that," I said. "But who the hell is Miley Cyrus? Wait, is she the kid on that *Hannah Banana* show?"

"*Hannah Montana*," Mario said. "See, that's why you need me. And you're going to have to start thinking about cutting back your hours and giving some of your clients to the other stylists."

"Okay," I said. "I'll talk to Sophia."

I worked on my kit orders in the back room all during lunch and any time I got an extra minute between haircuts. The day flew by. I finished my next-to-last client, and Cannoli and I walked her over to the desk. I looked in the book to see who my last client was. PITA was written beside the name in big red letters.

PITA is something you never want to see next to your name in the appointment book at your hair salon. It has only one meaning: *pain in the ass.*

I turned to look at the waiting area. The Silly Siren bride waved at me.

My heart started beating a mile a minute.

I looked down at Cannoli. Her blondish roots were starting to show. I'd grown careless.

Cannoli glanced over at the Silly Siren bride. I held my breath. Cannoli turned around and walked casually into the back room.

The Silly Siren bride still had baby fine hair and a fishlike mouth, but at least she wasn't dry heaving today. I decided to just play it cool and hope it was all a big fat coincidence.

"Hi," I said. "Cut and blow dry?"

She was carrying a great big leather bag, and she reached into it now. I thought she might pull out a weapon, maybe try to take Cannoli back at knifepoint. But she only took out a big white photo album.

She handed it to me. "I thought you might want to see the wedding pictures."

I couldn't think of another option, so I took the album from her. "Oh, right," I said. "How are you?" I flipped through a few pages, though I couldn't see a thing. "Wow, what a beautiful bride."

"The best hair I've ever had. I'm so coming to you from now on."

Cannoli must not have been able to believe her ears, either, because she poked her head out into the salon again. I caught her eyes in the mirror and tried to make her go back.

Cannnoli took a step forward.

I shook my head. My heart was pounding in my throat.

Cannoli took another step forward.

"She looks cute as a brunette," the Silly Siren bride said.

"What?" I said.

"We were so not compatible. I have this great Peekapoo now."

I closed my eyes and took a deep, cleansing breath. "I'm so happy for you both," I said.

The minute I got rid of the Silly Siren bride, my cell phone rang. I held it up and looked at the caller display. It was Craig. "Hi," I said.

"So," he said. "I'm moving out."

"Great," I said.

"I'd like to see you. You know, just to talk."

"No thanks," I said.

"Is it that guy from the wedding?"

"Nope."

"Then what?"

"It's you. You blew it, Craig, you know? I don't want to look back, go back. I'm over it. I want something more."

He didn't say anything. I picked up Cannoli and walked into the back room. I put her down and started putting kits together with one hand.

"Lizzie's coming home for fall break in a few weeks," he said. "I was thinking we could all get together."

"I know she is," I said. "She called me last night. She's bringing some of her friends with her, and I'm going to do makeovers for them."

"Maybe I —"

"Craig," I said. "You're not invited."

"Paesano!" I heard my father roar out front.

Cannoli yelped and went tearing out of the back room. I hung up on my ex-husband and followed at a slightly more dignified pace.

I was working on turning Sean Ryan into just plain Sean in my mind. It was a challenge, but I knew I'd get there.

"Hey," I said. I kissed him, even though the entire room was staring at us.

Sean handed my father a bottle of grappa and me a bunch of sunflowers.

"Hold the fort," my father said. "I'm off to date your mother." He held up the grappa. It sparkled in the late afternoon sun. "Holy cannoli, is this one a keeper, or is this one a keeper?"

I drank Sean in with my eyes. "Is the pope Catholic?" I said.

ABOUT THE AUTHOR

Claire Cook is the bestselling author of *Life's a Beach, Must Love Dogs, Multiple Choice* and *Ready to Fall*. She teaches workshops for aspiring writers and women coming into their own at midlife, and has had previous stints as a fitness teacher and dance and aerobics choreographer. She lives on the South Shore of Massachusetts, often called the Irish Riviera, with her husband, where they are occasionally visited by their borderline adult children and their laundry.

The employees of Thorndike Press hope you have enjoyed this Large Print book. All our Thorndike and Wheeler Large Print titles are designed for easy reading, and all our books are made to last. Other Thorndike Press Large Print books are available at your library, through selected bookstores, or directly from us.

For information about titles, please call:
(800) 223-1244

or visit our Web site at:
http://gale.cengage.com/thorndike

To share your comments, please write:
Publisher
Thorndike Press
295 Kennedy Memorial Drive
Waterville, ME 04901